STEPHEN ORAM writes social science fiction and is lead curator for near-future fiction at Virtual Futures. He enjoys working collaboratively with scientists and future-tech people – they do the science he does the fiction. He's been a hippie-punk, religious-squatter and an anarchist-bureaucrat; he thrives on contradictions.

He is published in several anthologies and has two published novels, *Quantum Confessions* and *Fluence*. His collection of sci-fi shorts, *Eating Robots and Other Stories*, was described by the *Morning Star* as one of the top radical works of fiction in 2017.

# STEPHEN ORAM

# BIOHACKED & BEGGING

SilverWood

Published in 2019 by SilverWood Books
Reprinted 2021

SilverWood Books Ltd
14 Small Street, Bristol, BS1 1DE, United Kingdom
www.silverwoodbooks.co.uk

ISBN 978-1-78132-857-6 (paperback)
ISBN 978-1-78132-858-3 (ebook)

British Library Cataloguing in Publication Data
A CIP catalogue record for this book is available from the British Library

Page design and typesetting by SilverWood Books

*Dedicated to*
*Gail Smith, Jane Walker, Paul Milnes and Penn Smith*
*for their invaluable help.*

# CONTENTS

# FOREWORD BY
# CHRISTINE AICARDI

'S[cience] F[iction] writers might then be understood as researchers, the authors of particular thought experiments that explore the questions their epoch is able to think and feel with, whatever the blocked, aggressive, constipated divides of the academic small world […]. They are certainly not able to bring reconciliation among the fighters, to bring peace where the science wars ruled, for instance, but the way they betray the respective versions of the hidden agenda those fighters have in common (as keepers of a truth besieged by illusions) might, if recognized, loosen the deadlock and irrigate the landscape with the blood of consequential ideas.'[1]

I came across this assertion by Isabelle Stengers not long ago and decided to make it mine. The irony is not lost on me that it comes from someone who like me is an academic, albeit in a different league entirely, and I relish its joyous ferocity against rarefied (figuratively and literally) academic debates. But more than that, I share the hope it carries about the role science fiction could play as a spillover effect beyond its literary and entertaining qualities – the hope that it could provoke fertile thinking about the technoscientific world we humans have created for ourselves, a world shaping us in return in often unexpected and unwelcome ways. Granted,

[1] Stengers, I. (2018). Science Fiction to Science Studies. In S. Meyer (Ed.), *The Cambridge Companion to Literature and Science (Cambridge Companions to Literature)*, pp. 25–42. Cambridge: Cambridge University Press. doi:10.1017/9781139942096.002

this doesn't sound very futuristic, contrary to what is commonly expected of science fiction. But then, science fiction has never been truly about the future. Even situated a long time hence in a faraway galaxy, it always speaks to the present of its writing. This is what Stengers encourages us to recognise and seize upon. This is also the premise of a couple of projects that Stephen Oram and I hatched and directed together (with the precious help of collaborators) between 2016 and 2018, out of which came some of the stories in this collection and in Stephen's previous collection, *Eating Robots*.

The projects enrolled science fiction writers, Stephen among them, to visit scientific labs and talk to scientists in fields as widely different as robotics, developmental neurobiology and genetic epidemiology. In both projects, the writers' brief was then to produce near-future fiction short stories inspired by what they had seen researched in the labs, stretching it out just a bit further into the world.

The stories had to be short enough to be read aloud as a springboard for discussion at public events that brought together writers, scientists from participating labs, commentators from various horizons, and diverse audiences.

For me, a scholar in social studies of science, the projects were the right opportunities for pursuing ideas I have become interested in: How good can near-future fiction be at provoking ethical and social reflection on emerging science and technology? How good is near-future fiction at mediating debates around such topics? Deeper and larger questions are churning under these interrogations, questions which so far academic approaches fall frustratingly short of measuring up to: How can we broaden the diversity of views effectively represented in setting the research agenda for science and technology? How can we encourage reflexivity in scientists and engineers? How can we engage diverse publics into concrete discussions of collective responsibilities around science and innovation?

Do not expect authoritative answers from me – I have none

to offer. Research wise, the projects were meant to be explorations that would, at best, suggest tentative hypotheses and alleys of investigation. They certainly did that, and I can share a few pointers.

First, about the public we attracted. A constant throughout the projects was that the public events we organised were over-subscribed, with very positive evaluations from audience and participants. An important message coming through their feed-back is that there is a public out there hungry for forums where they can explore the complex shades of ethical grey surrounding science and innovation, as opposed to the kind of purposefully orchestrated black-and-white debates so often taken to be the dominant norm of 'what the public wants'.

Second, about the writers who took part in the projects. What came out strong is the jarring contrast between the idealised and hyped visions of science filtered through science communication in the medias, and the reality of scientists' working practices – much more messy, low tech, repetitive and mundane than expected, not to mention burdened with all manners of bureaucratic and financial concerns. This closer-to-the-bone perception of scientific work and of the human behind the science was visible in several of the stories, which wove into their plots questions of research ethics, double binds and professional (mis)conduct.

Finally, about the adventurous scientists and engineers who opened their labs for us. From the perspective of encouraging their ethical and social reflexivity, the results are a case of a half-empty, half-full glass. Not so surprisingly, those who collaborated with us belonged to the already reflexive fringe, and the immediate reaction is, 'What's the point then? It's the less aware ones we need to engage with.' But I have come to think that reaching out to the more ethically aware fringe could prove to be an effective, although indirect, strategy in the long run. Because the more insular scientists do not take it so well to have non-scientists come tell them that they don't know best and should think more about the wider context of what they do, while they may accept it more easily when it comes from respected members of their own specialities.

So, why not think of the reflexive fringe, enthusiastic for the kind of engagement our projects offered, as relays for trying to reach out into the isolated corners of their fields? This is not an idle thought. Just skip to the end of the volume and read the comments that Claire Steves and Danbee Kim, two brilliant and dedicated scientists, have been inspired to write: we couldn't dream of best relays, could we? Besides, it seems that the most ethically engaged scientists and seasoned public engagement actors can discover new ways of thinking thanks to their encounters with near-future fiction.

A most rewarding moment in the projects was when one such scientist told me that although he had always been an avid science fiction reader, inspired and influenced by it, this had been mostly far-future hard sci fi, but his collaboration with us got him interested in near-future fiction, which he had been reading a lot more since, and he thought the best of it was especially good for bringing out deep sociological perspectives. He added that it had also triggered the realisation that what they were doing in his lab was turning fiction into facts, realising what had hitherto been only imagined: for him, the best stories are thought experiments, and as a scientist there is a responsibility in the choice of which imagined future to help turn into fact.

We are back full circle to the quote from Stengers that I started this Foreword with. So please, try to think about it and keep it at the back of your mind once you embark on the at times quirky, funny, dark and overall delightful reading of Stephen's stories. It may help you see hidden, dead serious depths behind the enticing stories. Enjoy!

Christine Aicardi
Senior Research Fellow in the Foresight Lab of the Department of Global Health & Social Medicine at King's College London

# BIOHACKED & BEGGING

'm trapped inside my head.

Surrounded.

Alone.

They said it would be like heaven, this Unified Sentience. No more speaking, just thinking. They said that sharing each other's thoughts would be the final step for humanity, the moment when true empathy was born. So, why am I sitting here on the street staring at the legs of passers-by begging for attention? Look at my skin. Dry, grey and cracked. Can you believe they genetically modified us to deteriorate when we lack flesh-on-flesh with other humans? It's for our own good, so they say. It stops us hiding our loneliness. I mean, what would happen with no physical contact? A mental meltdown? Well, that's the threat.

I immersed myself in this Unified Sentience once and the cacophony of crap that invaded my mind was crippling. I couldn't cope. In fact, I didn't want to cope. The tedious barrage of other people's thoughts was hell, not heaven. I'm not religious by the way, but these are the terms that come to mind. They promised a land of harmony and gave us a life of achingly boring noise. *Come on, join in. Don't you dare withdraw; we'll redesign your body to make sure.*

It was bad enough when we had the tech rammed into our brains. *You will listen to each other. You will empathise.* We soon hacked that. Turned it off or at least turned it down, but no longer. This ability to know each other's feelings and thoughts is now a part of my humanity, no longer tech. Great. We evolved. It's become an innate biological ability and it's a nightmare. There's no switching it off. You can only resist. And I do.

Day after day after day I come and sit on this same street corner. I hold out my hands, begging to be touched. I don't need them to look. I don't want them to connect, and I push them away with a torrent of nasty thoughts when they try. They back off soon enough.

They see my skin. They know I need flesh-on-flesh. A few brief moments and I'll last another day or so. It doesn't take much. The trouble is, they can smell the desperation. I can feel it in my head as they come near. Superficial hypocrites, emanating good thoughts about how nice the street is, the bountiful shops and their wonderful lives while hiding an undercurrent of sadness and loneliness buried beneath the trivial happiness they layer on in thick dollops. None of that alters the fact that I'm sitting here with my hands open and my sleeves rolled up.

Nothing. I've been here for hours and nothing.

A couple of children have veered towards me with warm thoughts of kindness and sympathy. Their parents grabbed them and walked a little faster to get away. They know what I need. A simple touch would help. They're scared of being infected by whatever it is that's dragged me down, petrified to let me into their heads. Not that I want to be in their heads or have them in mine. Absolutely not.

I shift position and the skin on my legs scrapes on the rough pavement. The pain is excruciating.

A woman kneels in front of me and grabs both of my hands. She feels my pain. She knows about Tim. I feel it in her too, the loss of a child, the ripping of life from where it belongs. We connect. She glances over her shoulder at her companion. A wave of their mutual love rolls over me and I feel my skin get a little softer. Without thinking, I send a pulse of gratitude back her way and she cups my face with both hands. Her companion wants to hug her to express admiration, but the woman won't allow it.

Instead, she channels the admiration from her companion to me.

I feel lighter. I feel wanted. I want to feel. My hostility trickles away. I don't want anyone crawling around inside my head. That's not what I'm after. I want... I want... I don't know what I want.

They link arms and continue their journey, touching others as they go, brushing their flesh against the flesh of their fellow humans.

Fleetingly, a man places his hand on my palm and my skin heals a little more. A child touches my arm with the tip of her finger and her mother doesn't stop her. I feel warm and fuzzy.

I don't want them inside my head. Not yet. Not for a long while yet.

Another touch. And another. And another. It's as if someone has turned on the tap and I'm sitting under a waterfall of goodness. A boy strokes my arm repeatedly while his father watches from a distance, sending waves of encouragement to me and his son. My skin is changing colour, becoming silver. I close my eyes and let him stroke. He's not my son, but... I can dream, can't I? You'll allow me a small moment of relief, won't you?

I feel his father step closer. I know his thoughts. *Yes. Yes you can, if that's what you need.*

# MR ENHANCEMENT

Mr Enhancement hands his white dress shirt to his assistant and flexes his back muscles. Two long lines of ears that snake their way down either side of his spine wiggle in time to the tightening and loosening of his body. His spine of ears broadcast the snap snap snap of his clicking fingers and the audience are enchanted. With remarkable dexterity, he runs his hands up and down his arched back and the crowd gasps at the horrific noise of hand on ear. Up and down he rustles; more and more they wince. He clicks a final click and then silence. His silence. Their silence.

He leans over his shoulder, smacks his lips in a kiss and they cheer. With one almighty leap he's halfway up the ladder to the tightrope. A second leap and he's there, clapping his hands behind his head for all his ears to hear.

One careful step at a time he edges out along the rope, balanced only by his outstretched arms. There's nothing between him and the adoring crowd below. He jumps, twists and lands facing the way he came. They roar.

He dislocates his arm and stretches awkwardly to stroke his spine of earlobes. The soothing sound calms the crowd and they fall quiet. Stroking. Kissing. He has them hypnotised.

There's a piercing crack as he tears his arm from its socket and throws it at them. Some laugh, most scream. He tears off the other arm with his teeth and casts it towards a different part of the crowd.

As he steps on to the ladder, he kicks them his left leg and hops to the ground where he bows until his back is parallel with the floor. Rapturous applause ripples along his exposed ears and the sheer force of appreciation reverberates around the arena.

His assistant clicks Mr Enhancement's limbs back into place and Mr Enhancement gives the crowd one last loud kiss over his shoulder before sauntering away waving his shirt in the air.

# DORMANT STATUS

'Alexa. Who is the most popular person in the world?' asked Nicole, even though she knew how her resident bot would respond because she was and had been for the past few years.

As she rubbed her daily dose of face cream into her skin, she cringed at how old and wrinkled she'd become. Thank goodness she didn't have to show her face to her public any more, one of the great things about being a social media star.

The blue ring around the top of the bot lit up. 'Gamila is the most popular person in the world.'

Slowly, Nicole screwed the lid on to the pot of cream and placed it on the shelf. This was a moment she had prepared for many times over the years, the moment when someone else became more popular than her.

'Alexa. Show me Gamila.'

A hologram of a young, dark-haired woman stared back at her from behind a posy of wild flowers.

'Alexa, find her location. I am going out.'

With a scarf wrapped around her face, Nicole ventured out into the night. It was an unfamiliar feeling, to be among people, and one she'd avoided as much as she could. Another reason to hate the young imposter, Gamila. 'Alexa,' she said to the microphone built into the hood of her coat, 'tell me where to find her.'

Alexa guided her through the streets until she could see the young Gamila sitting in the window of an upmarket restaurant surrounded by fans taking selfies. The perfect set-up for what Nicole had in mind.

Inside, the crowds made her even more uncomfortable. She pulled down her hood and unwrapped the scarf, hoping that the restaurant cameras were less sophisticated than the CCTV on the streets and wouldn't be able to match her as she was now to the old photos online. Step by step she got closer to Gamila, taking her time and making sure she didn't attract any attention that would result in being ejected from the establishment.

'Hi,' said Gamila as Nicole got to the front of the queue. 'A photo for your grandchildren?'

'Something like that,' said Nicole. She leant forward and put her arm around Gamila's waist. As she snapped the selfie, she injected Gamila with a needle so fine she didn't notice.

'Thanks,' said Nicole, and then she left the restaurant as fast as she could without looking suspicious.

Back in the safety and the comfort of home, she relaxed on her favourite leather sofa with a glass of Alcosynth.

The fun was about to begin.

'Alexa, show me Gamila's feed.'

The last entry was from four hours ago – a long time in the world of social media celebrity, especially since automated accounts had been made illegal. This was an era when you had to post for yourself or not at all.

Gamila had stopped. No warning or explanation.

Simply stopped.

There was considerable speculation about what had happened, with many commentators pretending to have the inside knowledge. But none of them were right.

That pinprick had sent microscopic nanobots into Gamila's bloodstream which had activated once she'd arrived at the specified location: her home. Nanobots designed to crawl around her body and gradually close it down, leaving her in a state of deep hibernation from which only Nicole could wake her.

'Alexa. Who is the most popular person in the world?'

'You are.'

# PUMPED-UP PRESIDENTS

The two presidents swaggered into the glass dome, one from either side.

The crowd, citizens from each empire separated by a transparent metal partition, cheered and jeered in equal measure.

President Putin waved a photo of her great-grandfather in the air and President Trump held the photo of his great-grandfather against his chest. Photos of the presidents who simultaneously, and some said with prior agreement, had made their positions hereditary.

Larisa scratched her nose, something she did when she was excited or scared. She was both. Tickets had been really hard to come by and she was ridiculously excited, but every time she pictured telling her baby son that she'd been at this momentous event, in person, she was hit by the fear that the world might not survive long enough for him to hear the story.

The presidents ceremoniously bowed and took off their shirts. They sat and stared at each other across the table with their skin glistening from the sweat of being fully pumped with enhancements and implants.

The psychological build-up to the negotiations had begun. There was a lot at stake. Energy resources were low and both empires wanted control of what little was left, either to sell at crippling prices or to hoard for their own. The fate of millions of citizens depended on these two champions and whether they could negotiate a solution. Alternatively, if their desire for global domination took over, a winner would have to be decided through a series of challenges set by the resident AI.

President Trump slammed his fist down and snarled at his enemy who, if the rumours were true, was his half-sister. President Putin smiled back with the characteristic twinkle in her eye that Larisa loved. Elbows were placed firmly on the table and they locked hands. The crowd erupted with applause; the warm-up rituals had begun.

Off to the side, tech teams moved sliders up and down to adjust the implants inside their champion's body. Enhancements that were limited to the rich and powerful.

The traditional handclap began slowly, gradually picking up pace until Putin slammed her opponent's arm on to the table for the third time. She'd won.

The surface of the table displayed what seemed to be two random sets of different coloured shapes, a puzzle. The tech guys went crazy, shifting the focus of the enhancements from physical to mental. Immediately, Putin started shuffling her pieces around with phenomenal speed and dexterity, glancing across to her tech guys every few seconds. Her citizens were whooping with joy. Larisa felt the bitter pleasure of being on the winning side. Sweat poured down Trump's face and the veins in his forehead were enlarged. His citizens were silent. He seemed confused, frozen as if he'd been paused. And then a grin appeared and his tech guys relaxed. Something had clicked. With a calmness that was starkly at odds with the topless sweaty president of the arm-wrestling, he moved his pieces with precision. An engineering diagram of an earpiece took shape. Cleverly, the AI had chosen something pertinent. It was the negotiator's number one tool – a nifty little device that instantly translated one spoken language to another. Essential, since each president had made a conscious and public decision not to learn the other's language.

A facilitator strolled across to the table and put an identical earpiece in the left ear of each president.

Putin opened the negotiations by punching the air and shouting.

Larisa couldn't lip-read and only the approved commentators were allowed to listen in, broadcasting their interpretation to the crowd through the official headphones. She tuned into Putin's channel. The commentator was spouting the usual drivel they resorted to when there was nothing to say, repeating the inevitable name-calling and self-congratulatory nonsense.

Boring.

Her attention drifted, searching the crowd for anyone she recognised or fancied.

Suddenly, the audience became agitated as the channels fizzed with the rapid-fire chatter of excited commentators. 'Unbelievable. Trump has the audacity to threaten to alter the weather and dry up our rivers. That's an act of old-fashioned war, surely?'

Putin raised her finger slowly, pointing at Trump's forehead. Larisa switched channel. 'She's reminding him they still have the old weapons, threatening to use them unless we sell them our wave energy at a reasonable price.' Putin mimicked the firing of a gun. 'And I quote,' said the commentator, 'comply, or we eradicate your citizens in a cloud of radiation.'

Larisa sat back, deflated. She'd hoped for more, hoped for at least an attempt to find a solution. She blinked rapidly to activate her lenses and tapped her wedding ring so it displayed a live hologram of her baby son at home, gurgling and without a care in the world. The poisonous commentary from her headphones made her feel sick so she switched them off and focussed on her baby. So cute. She wiggled her finger and he rolled around as if he was being tickled. Everyday life. Family. That's what mattered. Just as she was wondering if she should call it a day and go home, the crowd gasped. She looked up. Both presidents were serious and thoughtful.

She tuned in. 'I can't say for certain, but even with my limited understanding, I'd say it's faulty. It's not translating exactly what's being said. But hey, look at the result. They're compromising.'

She switched channels. 'This is a new angle from Trump. One that President Putin can work with. I've no idea what brought this on. It's transformative.'

Stillness settled across the crowd. What was happening? Neither commentator seemed to know. And the commentator who had spotted the faulty translations was saying they'd been fixed, but that a corner had been turned and remarkably the negotiations were continuing to be positive. The whole room was in a state of shock, staring at the two presidents shaking hands. Incredible.

A synthesised androgynous voice whispered through her headphones. It was a new voice, not one of the authorised commentators. She listened carefully. 'We are Occupy Babel, hacking for the future of your children.'

She clasped her hands, fiddling with her hologram ring. It seemed too good to be true, but if Occupy Babel were back, there was hope again. She hurried out of the stadium to head home. She had a baby to bring up.

# I AM BLUE

Arriving long ago from a distant place, I joined your rainbow, watched and waited.

Slipping out from the beautiful arc, I painted your sky and brushed your sea. I brought colour to your lives. Did you notice?

No.

An alien in your midst hoping for contact, yet you ignore me, mix me with others and dilute my soul.

My sadness permeates; you call it the blues.

# THE ENVOY OF THE
# ULTIMATE OBSERVER

Dear Ultimate Observer,

I've arrived safely and with little incident along the way.

Unless I hear to the contrary, I will investigate as usual and inform you of my opinion on the viability of this particular universe.

Unlike you, they are bound by linear time and organise their calendars in a way that closely aligns with the phases of their satellite moon, but not quite. That might be an indication of a dysfunctional need to try and tame nature or it might be a sign of a sophisticated understanding of your essence – that's something for me to determine while I'm here.

My pre-arrival research indicates that a handful of inhabitants understand that there are parallel universes which require an observer who is outside of time and space to make the ultimate decision on which universe survives.

As ever, I will report back to you regularly at intervals that fit with the world I'm visiting. In this case it will be once in every one of their months.

I am going to try something slightly different this time. I will publish my observations of them to them.

If they are able to understand and change as a result, this might be the one to favour when you make your final decision on which to keep and which to throw away.

Your loyal envoy,

Purpuraj Akcidento

# MONTH 1:

## You All Suffer

Yesterday evening I'd been sitting in my room watching the googlebox, soaking up your culture. I had just about recovered from a strange episode in a restaurant and it was time to venture outside again.

On the corner of the street I could hear the music, smell the sweat and see the company I craved. I opened the door, breathed in deeply and strolled over to the bar. A man wearing a flat cap nodded to me. I nodded back.

'Hello,' I said.

He smiled. 'Hi. New around here?'

'Yes.'

'Takes some getting used to. Me and the boys moved here thirty years ago and the locals are still deciding if we're allowed to be here. Eh, lads?'

A group of five men sitting in an alcove laughed. One of them banged the table with his hand.

'Bring him over here, Tommy,' he said.

'Can I get you a drink?' Tommy asked me.

'That would be very nice. Something small and strong, please.'

'Sounds like you need a tequila.' He beckoned the barman over. 'A Partida, the Elegante, please.'

'Come and sit with us,' called the man who'd banged the table.

I sat down and sipped. The tightness in my shoulders melted a little. 'Thanks.'

'No worries,' he said. 'If you don't mind me saying, you seem to have a purple tinge to your skin.'

'I don't mind. It's true. Doesn't bother you, does it?' I smiled and they smiled back, shaking their heads. 'I'm keen to find out a bit more about life around here and you seem like a nice bunch. Do you mind if I ask some questions?'

'Are you the cops?'

'Leave him be,' said Tommy, 'can't you see he's out of his depth. Being purple 'n all that.'

They all laughed and either slapped the table, each other or my back.

'Why do you farm living beings for food?' I asked.

'Come again?'

'I was in a restaurant and they offered me the flesh from a sentient being – a cow, I think they called it. I'm not used to it and I can't figure out why you eat some and not others.'

'It's the way it is. Some are born to be pets, some are born to be eaten and some are born to roam free.'

'Aren't you all the same?'

A smile slowly spread across Tommy's face. 'Nah. Some of us are much more important than others.'

'Not you though, eh, Tommy?' said one of his friends.

He carried on smiling. 'You see, Purple, if we didn't farm them, they wouldn't exist. There's a pecking order.'

'Think you're one of the free, do you?' said the barman as he collected the glasses.

'But why do they put up with it?' I asked. 'I'd rather not be born than suffer like that.'

'Ah. You say that, but we all suffer in one way or another, don't we? You can't get rid of suffering,' said Tommy.

Suddenly, I felt exhausted so I finished my drink and said my goodbyes.

Back in my room, I reflected on the conversation. The nub of the problem seems to be that although suffering is wrong, you can't avoid it.

Maybe the whole universe should be scrunched up and thrown in the bin?

Just a thought.

# MONTH 2:

## You're Deluded or I'm Confused

Until yesterday afternoon I thought I'd got a handle on you lot. But you never cease to surprise me.

You tell me there's a natural hierarchy and you're at the top. Well, that's not an unusual premise from the ruling class in any universe. The difference here is that you seem to believe that everyone down the 'food chain' is happy with the way things are.

Really?

You tell me that some are here to rule, some to entertain and some to be eaten; I wonder how many of you would swap places.

And you don't have to go too far down the ladder before you stop using names and just call them by their species.

It's wrong.

At least, that's what I thought until yesterday afternoon.

It was one of those sparkly afternoons and someone told me that the Heath was a pleasant place to get away from it all. There was a sprinkling of water on the grass and a fresh wind cutting across the lakes. It felt good. I was walking along by the side of a wood, admiring the lumps and bumps of the ancient trees. The rich smell of soil and moss hung in the air. I turned the corner and there were six couples walking along the paths that criss-crossed the green space in front of me.

I sat and watched.

Each couple was made up of one upper-class being and one middle-class being and it was the middle-class beings, the so-called pets, who were running around, leading the way.

Every now and again their companion would re-assert control by tempting them back with morsels of food.

And then I noticed something that blew my mind.

The middle-class beings were defecating wherever they wanted and their upper-class followers were scurrying around to pick it up as quickly as they could, congratulating them by saying, 'Good boy!'

I thought your class structure was pathetic and you were deluded, but now I'm not so sure.

Did I stumble across a weird fetish group on the Heath – an aberration – or is your universe more complicated than it first appears?

# MONTH 3:

## Babies with Bones Soft Enough to Eat

Last night I had to go out. I'd been on my own for too many days trying to make a decision.

My body is starting to fail. It needs more protein and iron.

You don't make it easy though. It seems my only choices are to eat someone or work out the complexities of combining non-meat foods.

I went to the bar on the corner and as soon as I walked through the door, the familiar smell of sweat and the thrilling sound of life being lived made my hearts beat faster.

The barman poured my usual pint of sweet dark beer and I strolled over to Tommy and his friends in their alcove.

'Hey, Purple. Haven't seen you for a while. How are you?' he said.

'Better for seeing you guys.'

'You look a bit pale, if that's possible.'

'My body's not reacting well to the food.' I sat down. 'That's partly why I'm here. I need some advice.'

'From us?' He laughed.

'Yes.'

'Lads, he needs our collective wisdom.' They stopped talking and focussed their attention.

'My problem…' I paused to think about how to explain it simply. 'My problem is that I need more iron and protein, but I can't eat your meat.'

'Eat spinach then,' said one of Tommy's friends.

'That doesn't work. In fact it has the opposite effect. I wish you grew meat in vats rather than insisting it comes from living beings.'

'That's disgusting,' said Tommy's friend.

'No it's not,' I said. 'We pay tribute to the original flesh donor every time we eat vat-meat. We respect and honour her sacrifice.'

'Vegetables and rice for you then,' said Tommy.

'But even the production of those causes a lot of deaths.'

'Yeah. But nothing that matters.'

'The lower classes?'

'Huh?'

'You call them insects and rodents.'

'Exactly. Not important.'

'What about fish?' asked Tommy's friend.

'They're sentient beings.'

Tommy's friend was getting agitated. 'For crying out loud, Purple. It's the natural order of things. Do you think they'd be bothered about eating you, given half a chance?'

'So many deaths just to keep me alive. It's not right. Look at that plate of food. Whitebait, isn't it?'

'Yeah. What of it?'

'I'd call it carnage. There must be a hundred dead beings on that plate.'

Tommy rolled his eyes. 'Maybe you should eat steak. That's only a small chunk of one being,' he said, accentuating the word maybe to stress his sarcasm.

'Good point,' I said, pointing at the plate of fish. 'At least the deaths per calorie would be small compared to those…those babies with bones still soft enough to eat.'

We finished our drinks in silence.

# MONTH 4:

## The Efficiency of Flesh

'What are you grinning at, mister?'

'Hello,' I replied.

Two girls sat down on the bench, one either side, and a third stood in front of me. I was staring at the commuters cramming themselves on to the steady stream of underground trains.

The evening before I'd been chatting with Tommy about the class structure, trying to find out more about why the upper classes run around picking up the excrement of their middle-class companions, their pets. He told me to have a look at the morning rush hour. 'They're not very sophisticated, you know. You should see 'em, packing themselves on to those cattle wagons they call underground trains.'

So there I was, sitting on the bench and grinning, as the assertive young lady had pointed out.

It was crazy. Thousands of the upper classes were shoving their way on to trains. Off to spend the day scurrying around and having every ounce of energy squeezed out of them. Off to earn enough money to make their frantic lives bearable. Embracing the madness so they can buy stuff to save them time and holidays to help them relax.

Have you noticed that those right at the top – businessmen, politicians and scientists – view everything as a machine? They see you as a widget that can be made to work better and better so they can win their global competition.

It's so different where I come from. We help each other become well-rounded holistic beings rather than driving each other to make our flesh more efficient. Although we do enhance our bodies with additional organs or redesigned limbs or even take drugs that make us better at what we do. But that's all geared to give us the time and space to nurture our souls.

The girl kicked me. 'Hey, purple man. I asked you a question.'

'I know.'

'You're weird,' she said with a mix of anger and fear. 'You purple weirdo!' She pointed at me and grinned. 'Selfie,' she shouted. They all laughed and posed as she turned and took a photo.

The other two deliberately jostled me as they stood up. 'Purple creep,' one of them shouted over her shoulder as they strutted along the platform.

They wouldn't know, but my purple tinge was the result of a failed enhancement. Nobody back home would have mentioned it. We know that sometimes experiments go wrong.

The girls disappeared round the corner and my two hearts slowed to their normal beat.

# MONTH 5:

## The Vicious and Stupid Upper Classes

It's taken me a few days to write this entry; Tommy made an accusation that sent me into an introspective tumble.

I met him last Friday to talk through an observation that was forming the major part of my report.

It was the middle of the day and the street was alive with the upper classes scurrying to and fro. Tommy was waiting for me next to a queue of them lining up to exchange their money tokens for food. 'Hi, Purple,' he said and held up a baby's bib with prison bars and *Inside for 9 months* printed on the front. 'Look at this. I love it. I've bought one for my niece. Make my brother laugh, that will.'

'Shall we?' I said, turning towards the coffee shop.

'Sure. This is all a bit mysterious, isn't it?'

'I need to talk something through with you.'

We stood in silence until it was our turn to order. 'Two double espressos, please,' he said. 'That's okay for you, isn't it?'

'Perfect. I need a clear head for this.'

'They'll be ready for you at the end of the counter,' said the barista, gesturing towards a square wooden surface with little sachets of sugar artfully scattered all over it.

We took our small cups of bitter black stimulant to the high stools in the corner.

'The thing is,' I said as soon as we sat down, 'I'm coming to the conclusion that the upper classes are stupid and, worse than that, they're deliberately nasty.'

'Don't hold back,' he said, sipping his coffee and chuckling.

'Tommy, let me finish. I have to make an assessment of this universe. Of course, I've only just started but first impressions aren't good.'

'Hey. You can make as many assessments as you want. It's your right to have an opinion.'

'It's a bit more than that, actually. Anyway, can I tell you what shocked me the other day?'

'Of course, but I'll have another of these if you don't mind.' He caught the barista's eye and held up two fingers. 'So what's got your goat then?'

'Goat, chicken, lamb… They wouldn't know, would they?'

He raised his eyebrows. 'What?'

'You eat crap. You eat cubes of unidentifiable flesh and you don't even care if it's not what it's supposed to be. But the problem as I see it isn't that you're eating a different species to the one you think you are. The problem is that you've set this whole thing up so you're totally removed from the harsh realities of eating each other. You know nothing about the food you're eating. In fact, it's only when something goes wrong that you're interested.'

He coughed. 'You're fixated on what and how we eat, aren't you?'

'It's a good way of getting into the psyche of a universe. And this one is not good. You eat each other and yet you're disgusted by the whole thing. Even those of you that don't eat meat keep themselves ignorant of the lower-class slaughter their food production causes. You're vicious and stupid.'

'Wow, Purple. That hurts. Is that really how you see me?'

'No. You and your mates have really welcomed me. You're great. I'm talking about the masses.'

'Let me get this straight. You think that humans are vicious and stupid?'

'Yes.'

'But me and my mates are okay. In fact we're quite nice?'

'Yes.'

'That's racist or speciesist, that is!'

He put his cup on its saucer, stood up, patted me on the back and left without saying another word.

# MONTH 6:

## Filth and Chemical Enhancement

A week ago we were sitting in the pub mulling over life, mulling over the universe, but mainly mulling over the latest guest beer and the apparent political swing to the right.

Tommy was busy convincing me I needed to see more of this world before making any judgements on it. 'What makes you think you know anything about anything?' he kept asking.

His friend, whom I'd not met before, was excited about a festival he'd been to every year for the past five years. 'It's a little cracker – less than five thousand people. You should come and have your mind opened,' he said.

'Tell me more.'

'It's four days in a tent in an alternative world.'

'Alternative world?' I asked. He'd caught my attention.

Tommy interrupted. 'You remember how freaked out you were by the daily grind of those commuters?'

'Yes…'

'This is their antithesis. Cool folk chilling out and enjoying the finer things in life.'

'Such as?'

'Music, beer and the open sky.'

'It'll broaden your horizons. Fancy it?' asked his friend.

'Sure. Why not?'

'Great. I'm Brian, by the way.' He held out his hand and we shook.

'Nice to meet you. They call me Purple.'

'I wonder why?' He laughed with a loud belly laugh. 'Meet us outside the pub at midday tomorrow. Just bring a sleeping bag and a tent.'

'A what?'

Tommy chuckled. 'Don't worry, Purple, I've got one of each you can borrow. Brian, we need to buy some stuff.' He gave me the thumbs-up as they left.

The next day I arrived a few minutes before noon and the six of them were already waiting in the back of a white van. 'Ready to party?' shouted Brian from the driver's seat.

Tommy shouted back, 'Take us to heaven.'

He closed the doors, the van started to move, and for the first few minutes, we all fidgeted until we were comfortable. The rain was smacking against the metal, giving the impression we were being pelted with stones, and every so often one of the lads would look at the roof and sigh.

When we arrived Brian threw open the back doors to reveal colourfully dressed families pushing carts and pulling bags through six inches of mud with the consistency of chocolate mousse.

'Gonna be a messy one,' said Brian loudly. 'As ever, eh?' he added quietly and smiled at Tommy. 'C'mon, lads,' he said to the rest of them as they climbed out and threw their bags over their shoulders. 'Here we go.'

We spent the first evening sitting on sections of tree trunks laid horizontally inside our circle of tents, drinking beer and laughing every time someone fell over.

As the weekend progressed, the children played with the mud more and more, slipping and sliding around, despite the desperate pleas from their parents to stop. The crowd slowly polarised into those that were enjoying the falling and the pushing and those that were uptight about it.

There was one guy who was caked from head to toe in dry grey mud. His long hair was matted into rope-like corkscrews and his equally filthy girlfriend was constantly pushing him over.

'Good morning,' he called whenever our paths crossed, no matter what time of day it was. I really warmed to his joy for life although for some reason he scared me a little too.

On the third day it was starting to look like your society was breaking down, with dirty strung-out people wandering aimlessly around piles of rubbish and half-eaten food alongside highly charged people scurrying about wide-eyed and seemingly on a quest for something that only they understood. I took Tommy to one side. 'Tommy. The mud…'

'Yes?'

'Some people are truly embracing it and some are revolted by it.'

'That's chemical enhancement for you.'

'They're enhanced?'

'Sure,' he said and chuckled. 'All part of the fun and it's the only way to deal with this filth.'

'Oh, I didn't know.'

Once I was safely home, I realised they'd been right and that the weekend had certainly been an eye-opener: there's a whole bunch of alternative people who are chemically enhanced to behave like children and who go out of their way to frolic around in mud and filth.

Using enhancement for such trivial pastimes would be frowned upon back home, where it's a very serious business indeed, and I don't know what to make of it.

The most amazing part of the whole weekend was that nobody, absolutely nobody, was nasty about my colour. There were quite a few expressions of awe and wonder, but for the first time since I arrived in this universe, I felt truly accepted by everyone I met.

That was mind-blowing and makes my next six months of observation far more interesting.

## If You Opt Out, You're Despised

Ever since my first meal, when I had to leave the restaurant without paying, I've been using Tommy's contacts to exchange my gold for money. Sadly, I ran out a few weeks ago so I had to find a job.

I applied for a lot of different positions related to the social sciences, all of which I was highly qualified for, and got quite a few interviews. It was horrible though. I'd arrive for the interview and they'd take one look at me and explain, slowly, that they didn't recognise my qualifications even though they'd accepted my application. In the two interviews I did have, I described my relevant experience and in one I even talked about what I'd bring to the company, but neither of them were interested.

After a few days of this, I sat down with Tommy to discuss my predicament. 'It's weird. It's as if they're deliberately misunderstanding what I'm capable of,' I said.

'Does that surprise you?'

'Of course. Doesn't it surprise you?'

'Not really. You've a lot to learn about prejudice.'

'Prejudice?'

'You're obviously not from around here. And you won't appear in their equalities tick lists so there's no compulsion for them to treat you fairly.'

'Cos I'm purple?'

'Mostly. Why don't you look for a job that doesn't require qualifications? There's a train company that's recruiting. Why not try them?'

I was desperate so I applied and got the job. Now I travel the country pushing a trolley up and down a train. Still, at least I get to meet a wide range of people and I get to see other parts of England.

Not surprisingly, having a job has prompted me to try and better understand the concept of money. It's weird. As far as I can work out, it's a way of using something with no intrinsic value as a proxy for something with actual value, such as gold. There are few places around the world that are allowed to produce it and they decide what it's worth; apparently it goes up and down in value due to circumstances that only a select few understand.

There are loads of places you can keep it and some give you back more than you gave them and some give you less. Bizarrely, most of them won't tell you whether it's going to be more or less before you invest – you have to gamble on their gambling. This seems to cause a lot of problems and on top of that someone else is having fun with your money!

In England there's a bank that sets the rate at which money increases in value – the interest rate. That's what you get back if you give it to one of their friends but it's worth less than it was when you gave it them. The time value of money, apparently.

It's as if they want to make sure you can't opt out of the system, making sure you're constantly working and dependent on the elite.

The sensible ones who seem to have opted out and don't enter into this saving and investment trap are pushed to the edges of society. They live one day at a time not knowing if they'll have enough money to obtain the food they need.

It seems to me that if you opt out, you're despised for taking the easy option, even though your stress is more real and more immediate than it is for the majority.

I'm not sure if I've understood your monetary system correctly, because it seems like complete madness to me.

## MONTH 8:

## You Need Empathy Drugs to Be Allowed Your Freedom

I'd been wondering what a truly liberal society would look like here, in your universe, so I was in the pub again, testing some fresh observations on Tommy and his friends.

In mine we're encouraged to hold our own individual views without judging anyone else's, but we have to take drugs that heighten our empathy to make it work. I wanted to get a sense of how liberal your world could be without these empathy enhancements.

It was late in the evening and we'd all had our fair share of alcohol when I introduced the topic. 'Guys, if you found fifty pounds on the street, would you keep it or take it to the police?'

They all groaned. 'Oh no, here we go again. More questions,' said Brian.

Tommy scowled. 'Leave him be. You should be pleased he's asking us and not asking some stupid politician.' A couple of them nodded. 'It's a good question,' he said, smiling at me.

'With a very simple answer. Keep it!' said Brian.

'That's all very well,' said Tommy. 'But the law says you should hand it to the authorities. Like that couple who found a winning lottery ticket for thirty thousand pounds, spent half of it and then got done for theft and they had to pay it all back.'

'Can I have a show of hands?' I asked. 'Who's for keeping it?' All six of them nodded. 'Even though it's illegal?' They all carried on nodding. 'What would you do if you saw someone drop the fifty pounds? Would you still keep it?'

One of them said no, but the other five, including Tommy, nodded again.

'Why is that different?' I asked the guy who'd said no.

'You know who it belongs to. But, if they were filthy rich, I'd probably keep it.' Tommy gave him the thumbs-up.

'What about stealing a wallet from a table in a pub?' I asked.

'If they're stupid enough to leave it lying around,' said Brian.

'And from their coat pocket?' I asked.

Brian snorted. 'Bit dodgy but yeah, if I had to.'

Tommy joined in the questioning. 'What about robbing from a house?'

'Very funny,' said Brian. 'You know I have.' He turned to the others and shrugged his shoulders. 'Only when a window's been left open though.' One of the guys got up and walked away.

'And mugging?' I asked Brian.

'If they're rich and cocky and you only threaten them, then that's kinda okay. They're probably some city slicker who's been robbing you blind in some legalised way anyway. You know – insurance, banker or something.'

'And would you hurt them if they refused?' asked Tommy.

'In self-defence I would, yeah.'

Tommy continued. 'So, you come across a rich, cocky old woman in the street who you know has been ripping people off for years as a financial adviser. Would you mug her? With violence?'

Brian didn't answer.

Tommy pressed him. 'Well, what would you do?'

'I'd try not to hurt her, but if she gave me no option then I'd have to, wouldn't I?'

'And if you came across her while you were robbing her house and she tried to stop you?'

'I'd walk away. You don't hurt an old lady in her own home, do you? You'd have to be sick to do that.'

I interrupted. 'Brian, why does it make a difference if it's in her own house?'

Tommy answered instead. 'We all draw a line somewhere, don't we?'

'But who decides where that line is?' I asked.

'You have to decide for yourself. You're the one that's got to live with it.'

'So, you decide what's right and what's wrong?'

'Yeah, I guess so,' said Tommy.

'If someone hurts an old lady in her own home that's fine by you, so long as they think it's okay?'

'No! Of course not.'

'So who decides?'

Brian put his pint down, gripped my jacket collar and pulled me towards him. He whispered, 'If some piece of scum goes too far, we deal with them. Get the picture?'

I lifted his hands off my jacket. 'I get it. There's one set of agreed rules, the law, but you have another set of rules that sometimes you impose.'

'Leave it there,' said Tommy. 'Who wants another drink?'

It was a fascinating conversation and I'm a little closer to understanding what a liberal world without effective empathy enhancements would look like. And I don't think it's very pleasant.

# MONTH 9:

## Unconscious Connections or Mass Manipulation

Tutting, shuffling and huffing: the bus queue showed its disapproval of the man smoking a cigarette. They shot him semi-furtive glances, but said nothing.

'What's the problem?' I whispered to Tommy.

'He's smoking.'

'Is it illegal?'

'No, but it's not very nice, is it?'

'Why does he do it?'

'Too stupid to realise it's the twenty-first century, I guess.'

'I don't understand.'

'Forget it,' he said and turned away.

The cold clean edge to the air contrasted beautifully with the cigarette smoke. On the roof of a café a metal chimney reflected the sun, like an urban lighthouse warning of the fatty smoke it emitted from burning flesh.

The bus arrived and the queue inched forward. We sat down in the last two empty seats.

'That's better,' said Tommy, unbuttoning his coat.

'Better than what?'

'I was starting to freeze to the pavement.'

I smiled. 'I could tell you were finding it hard to appreciate the crispness of the day.'

He stared at me, smiled and shook his head. 'Sometimes…' he said and took out his phone. 'Do you mind if I check this?'

'Sometimes…' I said, smiled back and shook my head in an attempt at humour, but he was too engrossed in swiping and pressing the screen to notice.

I sat back and looked around. Almost without exception the passengers had their heads down and their thumbs on phones. Occasionally someone would show a neighbour something, as if the virtual world was more interesting than the one around them.

'Tommy, these phones haven't been around long, have they?'

'Not really, no.'

'And yet they've taken over your lives.'

'That's a bit severe, don't you think?'

'Look around.'

'I see people on their phones.'

'What did they do before they had phones?'

'Well, they… Do you know, I can't remember. I guess they must have… Read newspapers? Talked? That's spooky. I honestly can't remember.'

He fidgeted, repeatedly taking his phone out of his pocket and putting it back almost straight away.

The bus trundled along, passengers got off and passengers got on, but their behaviour remained the same – heads down and thumbs swiping.

'We're here,' said Tommy. The bus was still moving, but he stood up and walked to the back, swaying as it weaved its way through the traffic. When it came to a halt, I followed him out on to a pavement full of couples and families walking slowly and frequently stopping to read the menus in restaurant windows.

'What do you fancy?' asked Tommy.

'I'll leave it to you. No meat or fish though. You know that, don't you?'

'Yeah, Purple, I know that. Wouldn't be right to eat your equals, would it?' He laughed.

I knew he thought I was wrong and that the lower classes were born to be eaten, but I didn't rise to his jibes. One day he'll understand my point of view. One day your whole universe will understand my point of view. But not until I fully understand you.

We meandered along the street, pausing every now and again for Tommy to check a menu.

'How do you decide?' I asked.

'Well, they've got to have a veggie option, haven't they?'

'Do any of them?'

'They all do. Actually, they're almost identical to each other.'

'Is that why you're looking inside as well?'

'Yes. You don't want an empty one, do you?'

'Why not?'

'There's a reason it's empty.'

'What sort of reason?'

'You can just tell that something's not quite right.'

It was fascinating to watch everyone choose where to eat, congregating in a few select places.

'Tommy…'

'I know that tone of voice… What have you discovered about us now?'

'The phones and forgetting what it was like before… The way you concentrate into a few restaurants without discussing it with each other… Do you think you're all connected in some way? On a higher level? Or are you being manipulated?'

He laughed and slapped me on the back. 'You're precious,' he said, but was silent for quite a while afterwards.

# MONTH 10:

## You Smell and I Like It

All sorts of smells pour out of your bodies.

You scrub yourselves clean at least once a day and try to disguise your odours with deodorants and air fresheners. You politely ignore the stink of your excrement as if it wasn't there. I know it all disgusts you, but I think it's your smell in particular that makes each of you unique. Where I come from, we're chemically altered at birth – our bodies simply don't produce anything that smells.

You have such a weird relationship with your bodies. According to the googlebox, you have a well-known phrase, 'beauty is in the eye of the beholder', which implies that other people choose whether you're beautiful or not. Another is 'beauty is only skin-deep', which implies your outer wrapper is the only part of you that can be beautiful and yet, conversely, you say that 'beauty comes from within'.

A few days ago I discovered that an extremely high proportion of your human females between the ages of eleven and twenty-one think they are judged more on their looks than their ability. A quarter of them have considered plastic surgery, something your popular media despises, while at the same time, and often on the same page, they promote physical beauty as one of the most important attributes you can have.

When I look at your magazines and your television and listen to your conversations, it strikes me that although you talk about beauty not being superficial, you don't really believe it. The amount of drivel that's pumped out about how someone looks is enormous and it extends to the middle classes, to beauty parades for your pets. It even extends to the lower classes, where in nature documentaries you describe birds and fish as beautiful and insects and rodents as ugly, which really reflects the amount you like or loathe them.

Why don't you let individuals decide their own form of beauty and let them get on with creating it, using technology to enhance themselves in whatever way they want?

I can see how altering physical beauty might be considered superficial, but if it wasn't for the pressure to conform, would it be that bad?

Although I have to declare self-interest. I wish you could accept difference more easily in the same way we do back home where my purple tinge is ignored. Here it attracts some unpleasant interest.

What confuses me is why you're against any form of drug or physical enhancements to extend your abilities beyond the so-called norm.

You place the beauty of the body on a pedestal as if it's the main passport to success, but then you vilify anyone who has the courage to use surgery to change the way they look. And you use massive quantities of drugs to alter your bodies for things you consider a sickness or a disability but have a *war* against their use to enhance life more generally.

Until you sort out these deep-seated hypocrisies, I don't see how you can progress.

And, although your debates on human enhancement are interesting and a few of you believe it's inevitable within a generation or two, you're a long way from understanding how the mainstream use of drugs and technology to improve yourselves will change your society.

In my view, coming from a universe where enhancement is taken for granted, I think your future hinges on how well you develop laws to govern its development and use – who gets it, who pays for it and who trials it.

I've set the ball rolling, as you say. I've thrown down the gauntlet and raised the flag up the pole.

I'm watching with interest and hope you work it out because I like you. And please, please, please learn to love those smells.

## MONTH 11:

*Celebrating the Magic and the Murder of Your Universe*

The sky was lit with multicoloured sparks and fires burnt all around us; Tommy had brought me to watch the city on its special night.

There was a sharp nip in the air but our own fire, burning inside the drum of an old washing machine, kept us warm. The flames flickered and the broken wooden pallets glowed.

'Isn't this great?' he asked.

'It is, but I don't understand. What's going on?'

'It's Guy Fawkes night. It's a celebration.'

'A celebration of what?'

'That's a good question. It goes back a long way, all the way back to the early seventeenth century when an Act of Parliament decided that on the fifth of November, we had to give thanks for the joyful day of deliverance.'

'Are you telling me that you have to do this by law?'

'Not any more – they stopped that in the mid-nineteenth century. But we carried on doing it anyway.'

'So what were you delivered from?'

'Guy Fawkes and his co-conspirators failed to blow up Parliament with their gunpowder plot.'

'I see. Was he a terrorist?'

'Sort of. He wanted to replace the Protestant king with a Catholic one.'

'Did they do that burning alive thing?'

'No, it's worse than that. They decided to hang him after cutting off his genitals and burning them in front of his eyes. They were going to do a load of other unpleasant stuff, but he managed to kill himself before they could do everything they wanted to.'

'And you celebrate this?'

'Yeah. Sick, isn't it?'

'I'm finding it hard to understand.'

In front of us an explosion of white sparks with tails of fire soared into the sky. As they reached the top of their arc, they burst apart. It was like a meadow of fiery flowers rapidly blooming in the night sky. The birth of each new spark was accompanied by a loud bang and as each one burst apart, the noise grew louder and louder. One by one the sparks shrank to nothing, leaving a mist backlit by street lights.

It became eerily silent.

'Wow, that was some spectacle,' I said.

Tommy lifted his finger. 'Wait and see.'

A deep boom bounced off the nearby buildings and the sky was lit by a ball of red sparks expanding outwards, leaving a black hole in their centre. They fell gracefully and silently. As they touched the ground, a set of six launchers pumped green fireball after green fireball into the air.

I whispered to Tommy, 'I thought they foiled the plot?'

'They did,' he whispered back.

'Why the fireworks then?'

He grabbed my arm and pointed towards the sky. 'Can't you just enjoy something for once?'

I nodded. I'd obviously upset him.

The cacophony of bangs and booms, the smell of smoke on the wind and the bright light of the explosions filled the air. Layer on layer of noise built up and built up, and then once again it subsided until it was silent and only the smoky mist remained.

I turned to leave, but Tommy caught hold of my sleeve. We stood for a few seconds. There was the most almighty boom followed by a dense cushion of tiny white dots and then bang after bang after bang as the sky filled with a blanket of white light and white noise.

It was exhilarating and frightening at the same time.

The aggression spilled out like a volcano of hate and I felt as if I was surrounded by the best and the worst of humanity; that cold night sky reflected the magic and the murder of your universe.

'You look stunned,' Tommy said as the crowd clapped.

'I am. I don't understand the symbolism of the fireworks.'

'It's a bit of fun.'

'Really?'

'Yeah, really.'

'Okay. Can I ask another question?'

'Of course. What's one more in your long list of enquiries?'

'Those protesters we saw the other day. The anonymous ones with the Guy Fawkes masks. Is that a Catholic revolution?'

He smiled. 'No, Purple. At least not as far as I know.' He patted me on the back. 'It's a confusing old world, isn't it?'

'Yes,' I replied and turned towards the fire.

It had been a beautiful and extravagant night, although it seemed strange to base it on so much pain and suffering, but then that does seem to be the basis for most of your celebrations.

# MONTH 12:

## You Need a Festival of Enhancement

'You're purple,' said Tommy's niece.

'He's from another universe. He came here to see how we live. Like a space explorer,' said Tommy before I had a chance to explain.

'But why is he purple?'

I put my cup of tea down on the sitting room table and beckoned her over. 'Where I come from, we change people so they're cleverer and stronger – we call it enhancement. Sometimes it goes a bit wrong and that's what happened to me.'

'Does it hurt?'

'No. Not any more. Do you like it?'

'It's cool. Will you help me?'

'Of course.'

She grabbed my sleeve and pulled me across the room to a child-sized green plastic table. 'Help me make some invites,' she said as she sat down on the matching chair.

I looked across at Tommy who nodded to let me know it was okay. I knelt down next to her. 'What's your name?' I asked.

'Lesia. What's your name?'

'It's really hard to pronounce, so just call me Purple.'

She giggled nervously. 'That's wrong, calling someone by their colour.'

I shrugged. 'It's what everyone calls me.' I rummaged through the cards, glue and glitter. 'Did you say you're making invites?'

'Yes.'

'Invites to what?'

'A party. Silly.'

I smiled. I love the directness of the young humans in your universe. 'But what's the silly party for?'

She chuckled. 'You're funny. It's not a silly party – it's a Christmas party.'

'Sounds fun.'

'It'll be great; lots of games, presents and cake. Shall I show you what to do?'

I nodded.

She scrunched her face with concentration and cut out some trees and some stars, glued them on to card and then sprinkled them with silver glitter.

'Do you have parties?' she asked.

'Of course, every universe I've ever visited has parties. It seems to be one of those things that happen wherever you are.'

'I bet ours are the best, aren't they?'

'I haven't been to many of yours, but I think the best ones are where I come from. Although you might find them a bit strange.'

'Really?'

'Yes. Shall I tell you about one?'

She put the remaining half-made invites in a pile and turned to face me with her chin resting in her hands. She glanced at the adults on the other side of the room. 'Go on,' she whispered.

I shifted a little closer to give her the impression that I was sharing a secret. 'Where I come from, we don't have Christmas but we do have a special party once a year – the Festival of Enhancement. There are lots of other parties and they're great fun, but this one is compulsory.'

'Does everyone go to the same party?' she asked with wide-open eyes.

'No. No. No. There's a lot to choose from and you only have to volunteer for one.'

She nodded wisely without really understanding, in the way that I realise is typical of you humans.

I beckoned her to come even closer and whispered, 'When we get to the end of the year, there's a list of all the new enhancements that have been developed. It tells you what they will do to you and which of the previous ones they can't be mixed with.'

'I don't understand,' she whispered.

'In my universe everyone has things done to them to make them better. We take medicine and have bits of our bodies altered to make us super-beings.'

'Oh,' she said, nodding wisely again. 'But what's that got to do with these parties?'

'Well, it's at these parties that they experiment with real beings to see if the new things work.'

She frowned. 'That's sad.'

'You shouldn't be sad – it's great fun. When you arrive they take you into a special room to do what they have to do and then we all sit in a big hall waiting for the changes to take effect. One by one it starts to work and you can see people experimenting with their new power.'

'What's yours?'

'Last year, just before I came here, I was given more empathy. That was amazing. As each change took effect on the others, I could sense what it was like.'

'Is everyone happy?'

'Even when it goes wrong, people are okay because we do it together and share the experience and there's no shame if it doesn't work. It only goes wrong on very rare occasions and someone has to be taken away. The festival organisers try their hardest to make sure the new one doesn't react badly with something else they've done to you, like turning you purple.' I winked.

'My dad takes pills to cheer him up but that means he can't drink beer. Is it like that?'

'Exactly, and in my world if you've had your brain enhanced, then you wouldn't be invited to the parties where your body is improved. When you're born, your parents have to choose between your body and your brain.'

She looked at me for a while and then looked away. 'Can we finish off these invites?'

I laughed. 'Of course we can, silly.'

She smiled and handed me the glue and the glitter.

Dear Ultimate Observer,

I have been here for one of their years – the time it takes for this planet to go around their star.

What can I say?

They are adorable, irritating, cruel and sad.

My assessment is that the humans are packed full of contradictions, particularly about enhancing themselves and their relationship to other species, but they're slowly evolving.

The amount of mind- and body-altering they indulge in while pretending they don't is incredible.

They promote the use of addictive stimulants such as coffee and alcohol and yet punish anyone who gets addicted. I think it's a minor issue, though, because when you study their history, you can see that the prevailing attitude around this ebbs and flows.

The major issue for me, and one that I think the majority are blind to, is how they treat the other species on their planet. In the main, they genuinely believe they love their fellow inhabitants, but because they are wedded to hierarchies, they simply cannot see their own cruelty.

It's as if they can hold more than one truth in their heads at the same time, which of course could be a sign of developing a higher order of consciousness. Possibly, and most probably unknowingly, tapping into the multiplicity of what they have labelled as Quantum Physics.

Would I recommend this universe as the sole survivor?

Obviously, it depends on what the others are like. If there's one where the humans are more equal to the other species, then my temptation would be to choose that one. However, I do think there's some potential here and I'd be sad to see it destroyed.

I'm happy to continue with my observations if that's what you require.

Your loyal envoy,

Purpuraj Akcidento

# EFFORT LESS

'Henry, you can tell a lot from someone's footwear,' his mother had been fond of saying.

He stared at his feet, lost in thought about his parents' prenatal decision to enhance him, the embryonic Henry, for a life of fully fledged privilege. A high-performing human. His shoes were scuffed, dirty and fraying where the plastic upper was coming loose from the sole. His whole body sagged with despair. Although, looking along the neatly lined up feet of the bus queue, his were no worse than anyone else's; public transport and poverty must be symbiotic, each dependent on the other. In contrast, a pair of handmade soft leather shoes stood a few feet away in the gutter. Nice trousers too, but why the hi-vis jacket and protective gloves? Aha, a streetcleaner. An extremely rich streetcleaner if he was willing to work in such expensive shoes. They lived in an effortocracy and no matter what Henry did or said would change that.

What a fucked-up world.

Despondent, Henry continued to wait passively in the queue which he suspected was almost entirely made up of the morning's appointments at the same assessment centre that he was being forced to attend. This poor struggling batch of humanity would be cajoled into behaving properly, to fulfil their potential. Made to acknowledge that they'd let themselves and everyone else down.

As the streetcleaner got closer, Henry activated his thumb-ring which interpreted the signals from the performance-monitoring chips implanted inside everyone's heads. For him, in his job as a surgeon, this wonderfully illegal present from his wealthy Uncle William was incredibly useful. Informing him of how much brain capacity people were using, it helped him gauge the ability of his patients to understand what he was telling them. Henry was actually a very good surgeon, but this gave him an effort-free edge that made his diagnoses superior to those of his contemporaries. The ring confirmed what he already knew from the streetcleaner's shoes – the guy was fully utilising his potential to do his job, every single drop of it.

The bus pulled up to the pavement, disturbing a puddle of rainwater which in turn drenched those oh-so-perfect shoes. Henry grinned. Poetic justice for being so crassly ostentatious.

Inside the assessment centre, he joined another down-at-heel queue moving with the deliberate plod that's characteristic of the unwilling heading towards the inevitable. A smartly dressed young nurse was waiting at the entrance to a cubicle. 'Good morning, Henry,' she said. He hated the familiarity they adopted as if it was theirs as a birthright. 'Step inside, please. We want to scan you for illnesses that might be causing your particular problem.'

Illness? What a joke. Boredom? Maybe. A huge dose of 'can't be arsed' for certain. But illness?

She opened the door. Sitting around the edge of the cubicle were three men and three women, all smiling. 'Please, step inside,' said the nurse. 'Between them, they can sniff any illness at three metres so don't worry, we'll soon see if you've a problem.'

What was the name of that bloody woman, the one they'd discovered could smell Parkinson's disease on someone before the medical tests could diagnose it? Joy Milne. That was it. It'd taken them a while to work out how to reproduce her gift, but once they'd cracked it, men and women had flocked to be medically engineered. With the capability to smell disease, they'd snapped up the jobs that came with the enhancement.

The six sniffers twitched their noses for a while and then shook their heads. 'All clear,' said the nurse. She touched his elbow and pointed. 'Down there and left at the end.'

There were two assessors. The one who had some spare brain capacity would be the preferable of the two so he veered towards the scruffy one, hoping he'd guessed correctly. Annoyingly, the smartly dressed one beckoned him forward.

'Henry.'

There it was again. That impertinence. Using his first name as if they were best buddies.

'Please...take a seat. My name is Mr Clarke.' Mr Clarke was busy stroking his screen. 'I see your genes were altered before you were born. All those inconvenient errors corrected,' he said without looking up.

'Yes. And your point is?' replied Henry.

'Well,' said Mr Clarke, 'judging by your performance results, I'd say it was a complete waste of money. You don't use anywhere near your full potential in your work.'

'I do a good job.'

'True. And you could do an amazing job if you could be bothered.'

'You pay me accordingly, so what's the problem. Being poor is my choice not yours.'

'We want to help you make the most of yourself and if you don't we will keep reducing your pay until you see the error of your ways. Unless...' Mr Clarke swiped his screen again. 'Are you suffering from depression? We can test you.'

'My family doesn't do depression.'

Henry wished he'd got the other assessor. This guy was only just coping, pushed firmly against the ceiling of his capabilities. No chance of a conversation with this one.

'In that case, Henry, I have no option but to apply another sanction. A further five per cent cut in your wages. Effective immediately.'

Henry stood up. There was no point in arguing or trying to

make this guy see sense. If only he could perk himself up a bit when he was at work and stretch himself a little. Why bother though. He did a good enough job and it left him plenty of energy for other more pleasurable things.

Outside, the grey clouds drifted aimlessly across the sky. He had an idea. In his original damaged state, his potential was less. An un-enhanced Henry might have been able to find the effort required to earn a high salary. His only hope was undoing those embryonic alterations. Reversing repairs was costly. It would take a long while to save up enough from his wages. He could work longer hours. He could even push himself harder. The thought made him shudder. He stared at the clouds. They looked so calm and relaxed as the wind gently moved them across the sky. There must be an easier way than working to get the money he needed. Something that didn't require so much…effort. He needed a benefactor. It suddenly became blindingly obvious. Uncle William had a substantial income from the old family investments. And he was a decent chap. Yes. Uncle William was certainly worth contacting; undoing those genetic fixes might be just the ticket Henry was looking for and Uncle William could be the very man to help.

He made the call. 'Hello, uncle,' he began. 'How are you?'

'What do you want?'

'Well…'

'Get on with it, boy.'

'I was wondering if you can lend me some money to pay for an enhancement reversal.'

'Lend you money? Not in a thousand years.'

'But you're not short, are you? And it's for a good cause.'

'I paid for the darn things in the first place. I'm not paying to have them removed.'

'If you do, I can earn more money. I'll hit my effort ceiling much easier.'

'Put in the graft like everyone else and save up.'

'But you can help me shortcut that. I'll get money sooner and pay you back quicker. Everyone's a winner.'

'You're not borrowing, so there's nothing to win.'

'It's not like you worked hard for it, is it?'

'It's a lot of effort to keep hold of it with the likes of you around.'

'Not real effort though, is it?'

'Ha. Don't you believe it.'

'You're not monitored, are you?'

'Irrelevant. Now get off the line and get on with earning your own money. Goodbye.'

Henry sat down on the pavement with a thud. Picking at his frayed shoes, he contemplated his options, knowing he would spiral down and down until he could no longer afford to even travel to work, knowing his options would be begging or a black market reversal. He shrugged his shoulders, stood up and sauntered home to the only escapism he could afford – sleep.

# RECONNED

I t was Sunday, early in the morning and they were having breakfast. Family time was precious and this was the only sacrosanct meal of the week where they were all guaranteed to be at home – him and his wife, their son Junior and his seventeen-year-old James. A drone disturbed their sanctity, knocking loudly on the door to announce the delivery it had left in the porch.

The parcel, a reconditioned ex-military robot configurable to protect his family's health, was from a second-hand bidding site. As far as he could see, the only difference to the more expensive reconditioned ones was that it was from a private seller rather than an established shop and he had no idea why anyone would pay triple the amount for a new one.

He'd been waiting for it to be delivered for some time and as soon as he could he took it down to his workshop, unpacked it and carefully laid it out on the bench. Tucked inside underneath the bot were the instructions. He unfolded them and despite the bad translation he painstakingly worked through each step. After entering strings of random characters, codes for this and that, and pressing a series of buttons – in the right order of course – he uploaded the family photos so the bot knew who was who. The final instruction told him to enter the factory code from the inside of the packaging so it could configure itself to the specifics he'd purchased – a preventative healthcare system that would monitor his family's health for danger signs.

James had been pestering him for ages. Pointing out that by spotting problems sooner rather than later it'd save money on health bills in the long run. And, if he was honest with himself, he was relieved to have finally bought one. He entered the code and waited, pondering on the preventative element of his purchase. There were cheaper health bots but they only cared for the sick or administered medication. This one was more specialised.

The green light on the side of the bot lit up. It was configured.

He took it outside and let go of it in mid-air. It hovered for a while and then shot up high above the house. It was designed to roam freely, making its own decisions as it went.

Junior's friend had arrived and they were splashing around in a plastic pool. What fun they were having. As he stood watching them, a bird in a nearby tree was singing its wonderful song. He laid his hand over his heart. This was the perfect Sunday.

Junior screamed. The other child had bitten him. Whoosh! The monitor-bot flew over his head and fired. A searing bright light hit Junior's playmate.

The child screamed; his lips were like molten wax dripping on to his chin.

The next few minutes were a blur. He rushed over to Junior. Somewhere in the background, his wife was screaming. Junior was screaming. The child was screaming. His wife was talking to someone on the phone and after what seemed like only seconds, loud sirens and blue lights filled the air.

He was taken away by the police.

The company he'd bought it from took no responsibility; it was in the small print. And he'd been the one that had entered that final configuration code so he was the one they charged – assault by activating an autonomous deadly weapon.

# SYRUP AND CIGARETTES

Screaming white noise. Pitch-black darkness. What a way to be greeted into a new day.

Aiden felt around for the edge of his cardboard mattress. Beyond its frayed borders buried among the food scraps and his few discarded clothes was the syrup he craved. The withdrawal was intense as the nanobots issued their friendly warning that his addiction needed feeding for him to stay alive.

Fumbling around in the detritus of his life, he found his last vial of bot-syrup and gulped it down. A pinpoint of bright light appeared. Then another. And another. And another. He blinked. The nanobots were working. A gradual shift from the oppressive white noise to the welcoming sounds of a city going about its daily business.

As his sight returned, he noticed the clock on the house control unit in which his robot waited while he slept. 'Jessie, why didn't you wake me? I told you – 7am.'

'Good morning, Aiden. It was in your best interests to sleep longer. Your metabolism needed the rest.'

'Don't you do what I tell you any more?'

'Not if it would cause you harm.'

'For fuck's sake. Being late for these lunatics will cause me more harm than a little tiredness, you stupid robot.'

'Would you like me to cancel your appointment?'

'No.'

Aiden sat on the edge of his bed rifling through his clothes desperately trying to find something wearable. Everything was dirty, but he sniffed each item and gradually pieced together an outfit for the day. Maybe after today's transaction, he'd be able to buy a pure water bath to reactivate the self-clean molecules in his clothes.

'Jessie?'

'Yes, Aiden.'

'It's best to play safe today and inhabit the old female body.'

Jessie transferred from the control unit to the mother bot, as Aiden affectionately called it. With Jessie at the helm, the mother bot shook off the junk piled on top of it and stood up.

He lifted the top four layers of his corrugated cardboard bed and took out a bag of vials wrapped in an old rag. It would be delicious to keep a couple of the sweet bot-syrup vials, but he was a mere delivery boy and even his addiction couldn't overcome his fear of his supplier or today's customer. He handed the bag to Jessie.

'Aiden, it's illegal for me to carry this.'

'It's black market.'

'It's illegal.'

'Just carry the bloody thing.'

'I have stored a copy of you issuing that instruction to protect myself from decommissioning.'

'Let's go,' he said, more to himself than Jessie, who would follow him wherever he went.

The streets were packed with humans going about their business, each accompanied by their own unique-looking robot following half a step behind. 'Whatever happens with these guys,' said Aiden to Jessie, 'you must protect me.'

'Understood,' said Jessie.

'Who knows what harm they might do to me if they're not happy with the goods. It'll be more than refusing to pay, that's for sure.'

'Understood.'

The door to the gang's offices was conspicuous by its failed blandness. Painted dark battleship grey, it was criss-crossed with STF-filled plastic bars down its length. Bars that would instantly harden if forced. Aiden knocked. The tiny speck of red light above the door let him know that someone inside was watching. He waved. Jessie waved too. 'Remember. My life is in your hands,' he said quietly.

With an over-engineered creak, the door opened and the sound of a violin concerto drifted down the hallway. 'Mendelssohn E Minor Opus 64,' said Jessie matter-of-factly.

Aiden fixed his smile and walked towards the source of the haunting music. Beautiful in normal circumstances, but somehow made sinister by the setting. 'Pass me the bag,' he said to Jessie.

Through the smog of highly illegal cigarette smoke, he could see the silhouettes of the gang members lost in the euphoria of syrup and music, each cradling a knife across their chest. Their leader, who was standing watch, swaggered over to Aiden. He gave her the bag and she offered him a cigarette. The precious hand-rolled cylinder sat in the palm of his hand; it was only the second time in his life he'd been offered one.

Jessie took the cigarette from him and crushed it to a pulp. 'Smoking kills.'

All heads turned towards them.

'Shit,' said Aiden. 'Sorry. Bit of a misunderstanding. These robots, eh?' He laughed a hollow laugh.

The gang leader stared at the crumpled mess in Jessie's hand. 'Expensive mistake,' she said as she ran her thumb along the sharp blade of her knife. 'Aiden, isn't it?'

He nodded.

'Leave,' she said. 'Leave now.'

'The syrup?' he asked.

'Thank you. Appreciated.'

'Payment?'

'Get out,' she said quietly. 'Now!'

She turned to the nearest gang member. 'Terminate that robot,' she said, looking at Aiden for confirmation. When he didn't reply, she took a step closer to him while rubbing her blade against her leg. He gulped, looked at Jessie and nodded his agreement. Jessie adopted a fighting pose; she was equipped to maim and kill if necessary. The gang leader took another step closer to Aiden.

'Protect me,' he shouted.

Jessie knocked the bag out of the gang leader's hand and the vials of syrup spilled out on to the floor. An unconvincing smile formed on Jessie's lips as they emitted a high-pitched whine, triggering a few of the vials to emit an orange glow which was followed quickly by a puff of black smoke. They were destroying themselves. The gang leader dropped her knife and scrabbled around on the floor, desperately trying to gather as many as she could.

'Shit and double shit,' said Aiden.

Jessie grabbed his hand and dragged him out of the building.

'Enemies for life,' he said as they walked away quickly. 'No money. No escape.' He turned his head. 'Your stupid robot rules. I'm as good as dead.'

'I will protect you,' said Jessie.

# CAPITALIST CRUMBS

Dave inched his way towards the perimeter fence. His ribs scraped along the mud and over the weeds as he dragged himself along. He was starving. Everyone was starving. They were victims of yet another war between the corporations. Brian, his best friend and comrade in arms, was inches to the left, tears streaming down his face from the pain.

'They've got drones, you know. Bad ones,' whispered Brian.

'They don't. It's a rumour.'

'Even if they don't, stealing is illegal, with severe punishment during a war.'

'Their war, not mine,' said Dave as he reached out to touch the fence.

'That may be true,' said Brian, 'but the war is crippling their profits.'

'I know the speech. Zero tax from them, no basic income for us.'

'Exactly, we're in it together.'

Dave spat into the mud. 'Shut up, and shove your loyalty card...'

Brian opened his mouth wide and closed it slowly, as if he was performing in a pantomime.

Dave grinned and Brian grinned back.

In the distance, beyond the landscaped lawns and the carefully tended trees, was row after row of driverless trucks parked in front of a warehouse. The monolithic monster of unfettered consumerism stretched into the distance in every direction, appearing as unbreachable as capitalism itself.

'Here,' said Dave as he handed Brian a balaclava. 'Put this on and activate your suit.'

Patterns that mimicked grass, tree roots, foxes and badgers flowed across their clothes. In theory they were now unrecognisable by any algorithm, drone or otherwise.

Inside the warehouse in the controller's office, Gemma and Anne chatted while watching a multitude of robots whizz up and down the long aisles, counting, picking and packing the produce growing in the artificial atmosphere on the other side of the glass wall. Behind them was a graphene bench that displayed whatever Egghead decided they needed to know about its inner workings. Egghead was the charmingly named artificially intelligent neural network that ran the entire facility. Gemma pointed at the bank of CCTV screens to their left. A couple of those that monitored the outside of the warehouse had flashing red borders, but the letters along the bottom were just a jumble struggling to form a word.

'It can't decipher what it's found,' said Anne.

'It'll be UBI scavengers for sure.'

'Probably. It's seen something. If—' Gemma halted mid-sentence, leant across to the graphene bench and laid both palms flat on its cold shiny surface. Clusters of holographic images emerged, spinning and moving as if they were alive.

'What?' asked Anne.

'Look. There. Egghead is changing again,' replied Gemma.

Anne swung her chair around so she was closer. 'Attack?'

'It could be.'

They swept their hands above the dark surface, hovering over the occasional word cloud before continuing with their search for an answer.

'It's changing,' said Anne. 'It's definitely changing.'

'Yeah, ignore that UBI scum. The competition has hacked their way in again. They're streaming false information into our datasets.'

Anne leapt up, shoving her chair back. The crash against the wall echoed off the hard surfaces of the room. 'They've already stopped the trucks from driving. What else can they do?'

Gemma pointed at the bench. 'Look. News stories about people being locked in driverless trucks and left to die are flooding into Egghead.'

Anne stared at the word clouds. 'There's another,' she said. 'Rotting piles of food incarcerated inside the trucks.'

Egghead was busy assimilating the news into its data store, unaware that it was consuming fake information as if it was real.

'I wish Egghead wasn't so stupid,' said Gemma.

'Me too,' replied Anne as she swept her hands across the bench, trying to counter the attack.


Outside, Dave and Brian inched their way forward while the fabric of their camouflaged suits and balaclavas spun a web of deceit.

'It's amazing they can't see us,' said Brian. 'I can see you perfectly.'

Dave shrugged. 'They're not that intelligent.'

'And yet we're the ones who suffer.'

'Yeah, a war with no direct casualties waged by algorithms that only care about the corporation,' muttered Dave, not expecting an answer.

The silence of the night was broken only by the wind in the trees and the staccato calls of foxes.

They crawled along, both of them wincing with the pain of the ground against their bones. Dave glanced at his watch. 'Soon,' he said in a hushed tone.

'Soon?' whispered Brian. 'Soon?'

'Tip off.'

The air was filled with the sound of several tailgates opening.

'It's time,' said Dave as he stood up, poised to run across the grass. He tossed a small disc to Brian. 'It'll operate the crates in the trucks. Grab what you can,' he called over his shoulder.

A swarm of drones came swooping down from the roof of the warehouse. They hovered with their guns pointing at the trucks as if they were waiting for something or someone to appear. Nobody did, but nonetheless they hung there. Waiting.

Dave ran past them, shouting. 'Brian, it's okay, they can't see us. Come on, grab as much as you can.'

Piles of soft berries had spilled out of the back of one of the trucks and they devoured a handful before pressing their discs against a dozen of the crates neatly stacked inside.

'Let's go,' shouted Brian.

They ran across the tarmac to the neatly cut lawns and then on to the border fence. The crates followed them, floating a few inches above ground.

As soon as they were under the fence and out of danger, they pulled off their balaclavas and their camouflage suits.

'This way,' said Dave.

'Wait,' said Brian, catching his breath. 'Who sent the disc? Why did they help you?'

'In war, propaganda is king. If the shareholders believe their auto-corp can't even protect its own goods, they'll sell up, destroying the corporation. At least I think that's the idea.'

'And in the meantime we wait and starve.'

'Not for a few days at least,' said Dave. He wrapped his arms around his friend and gave him a big hug. They laughed and hugged and jumped up and down on the spot. They'd done it.

Without Dave or Brian noticing, the crates silently lifted off the ground, hovered for a few moments and then slowly slipped away. Controlled by an unseen master.

# THE QUEEN'S HEART

'What do you mean, there's nothing more she can do? She's a doctor for fuck's sake, doctor to the Queen of fucking England.'

'Excuse me, madam. Would you kindly desist from swearing in front of Queen Ariana,' said the queen's private aide.

'The queen is unconscious, you idiot.'

'Nevertheless.'

'Aw, did I offend your sensibility. I'm so sorry. Go and tell that so-called doctor, that waste of taxpayers' money, to come and fix the fucking queen.'

'The doctor has already told you, there's nothing more she can do.'

'Look here, you overpaid lackey, do you remember what Ariana said about me and you?'

'Yes. You have her full authority and I am to obey you at all times, unless she says otherwise.'

'So, shut up.'

'The doctor told you, the queen has cancer. It's about to spread and she can't stop it.'

'Bullshit. Why can't she inject another one of her potions into Ariana's blood and stop it shooting those shitty cells all around her wonderful body?'

The aide stepped forward and lowered her voice. 'Madam, I realise you're upset. I know you and the queen are…close.

But, I must insist that you follow the protocols and stop your foul-mouthed utterances.'

'Tits to you and your prissy protocols. Remind me again, who employs you?'

'The trust fund set up by the queen's mother and father.'

'Well they're dead and I'm wrapping up the fund, so you're defunct. As from now, you're out of a job and homeless.'

'Well, really! I must protest.'

'Go away, Queen's Aide, before I have you removed. And I will. You know I will. And send that fucking doctor in.'

The sharply dressed aide ran her fingers through her grey hair. 'The queen's bit of rough,' she said under her breath. She turned on her perfect four-inch heels and left the room.

'Click clack click clack. Heels, I ask you? This country, it's barbaric. Cut off from the world. Isolated. Living in the faded glory of its past. I'd get the hell out if it wasn't for her, my queen. Right then, doctor, now that tight knickers has retreated, tell me, what's the score?'

'I've told you many, many times. There's nothing more I can do.'

'Yeah, I know, but now the protocol princess has gone, you can tell the truth. What's the latest cutting-edge treatment this island has to offer? Money's no object; the taxpayer has deep pockets.'

'Those tiny nanobot molecules have done all they can; they've found the cells, delivered the drugs, but it hasn't worked. All the signals coming back from the bots show that the cancer cells are about to invade the bloodstream. There's nothing more we can do.'

'What about Mairi Glass at the Elsa Berg institute? She figured out how to communicate with cells years ago. Sweden even has laws about it.'

'No. She's a quack, a dangerous quack.'

'I went to the centre with Ariana. We loved her. Amazing stuff. They were persuading organs in this guy's body to accept a cybernetic heart. She reckoned the organs were plotting to remove it, to reject it, which, as she explained, was very short-sighted of them because without a heart they're all fucked.'

The doctor stood there, staring.

'Wind your neck in, please. Anyone'd think I'd suggested voodoo or exorcism.'

'Please,' the doctor whispered, 'don't validate this in any way. If word gets out that the queen is having this treatment, it'll become the norm.'

'Typical protectionist crap. Look at her, my beautiful lover, my queen. You've got nothing for her so don't presume you have any say over what happens next. Get out!'

'It's illegal.'

'Get out!'

The queen lay on her bed surrounded by machines and monitors. On either side of her bed was a large electromagnet.

Mairi's team had arrived a few hours earlier and now they sat quietly, occasionally pointing at something or making complex hand gestures. The silence was comforting in an odd sort of way. They were learning the language of the queen's heart and it was taking a very long time.

'Can't you just get on with it and tell those bloody rogue cells to stop pissing about and die.'

Mairi folded her arms serenely. 'We're almost ready. We know what we're doing; it's standard practice back home, especially for cancer cells. I know she's precious to you, but one false move in this negotiation and we could cause more damage than good.'

'It'll be too bloody late by the time you've worked out how to be at one with the organs. Maybe the doc was right.'

'Patience,' said Mairi. 'We have to learn the language of her particular heart if we're going to persuade it to negotiate with the complex mix of water, proteins and neurons to block the cancer cells from entering the blood. Ultimately, it's in all of their best interests so it should work.'

'Tits. I wish I'd never called you. Look at her. It's fucking embarrassing to see her like this.'

Mairi continued watching, hand-signalling to two of her team who were drawing symbols on the large screen at the side of the room.

At last they all stopped and faced each other. 'We've made contact,' said Mairi. 'We said hello. The heart said hello back.'

'What the fuck do you mean, you said hello?'

'We've recognised each other's existence. Now we will negotiate.'

Two of the team stood by the screen while another two faced the monitors. Mairi sat beside Ariana and held her hand. 'Go,' she said.

The bots streamed information back to the displays and the two scientists called out an undecipherable set of numbers and characters to the other scientists who scribbled away at diagrams and formulae, calling back to their colleagues once they'd done whatever it was they were doing.

'What the hell is going on? What are you doing to my queen?'

Mairi beckoned her over. 'Here. Come and hold her other hand.'

They waited.

The scientists watched, scribbled and sent a pulse through the electromagnetic field. Then watched some more and pulsed some more. For what seemed like hours they pressed on, watching and pulsing until one of them laughed.

Mairi laid the queen's arm across her chest. 'We've done it,' she said. 'The cancer cells have given up trying to get into the bloodstream.'

'Have you fixed her?'

'We have for now.'

'For now?'

'Yes. Give us time and we'll try to persuade the cancer cells to leave for ever.'

'Time? We don't have time.'

'They're contained for now.'

'For now?'

'We can do more, but there's always a risk of a failed negotiation and an unexpected reaction. Do you want us to continue?'

'Yeah. Fuck. Go for it.'

'Okay. We'll need an old one.'

'Old one?'

'Old person.'

'What the fuck are you saying?'

'We use volunteers, near the end of their lives, as hosts.' Mairi screwed up her eyebrows. 'We fool the cells into thinking it's a new home.'

'Shit. Shit. Let me think.'

'The sooner the better.'

'Okay. You, yes you guarding the door. Find that old decrepit aide and bring her to me.'

# ZYGOSITY SAVES THE DAY

'Will she recognise us?'

'Oh, Isabella, I don't know.'

'I hope she does. I'm not sure how I'll cope if she's in a state again.'

'She's your mother, you'll cope.'

The two women made their way through the snow, carefully avoiding the slush and the ice, and whenever they reached a particularly hazardous spot, Lara grabbed her niece's arm for support.

They stopped at the tall iron gates to the grounds of the ancient building and Isabella smiled as the camera swung around to face them. She nudged her aunt. 'Smile,' she said. Isabella felt Lara stiffen. 'It's okay, auntie. It's only facial recognition, it's nothing sinister.'

'I know,' said Lara. 'I'm not used to these public health facilities; things are more subtle in my private one.'

The snow was fresh and crisp and the crunch underfoot was a welcome distraction from the ordeal ahead. With the wind blowing across the fields and through the trees causing a loud rustling like a stream running over rocks, they left a trail of footprints behind them as they walked along the track to the old house. A large clump of snow fell from a branch on to the path in front of them and they both faltered briefly before continuing.

Isabella broke the comfortable silence. 'Why her? Why did she end up like this?'

'Because, just because,' said Lara quietly.

Isabella was angry and didn't hide it. 'I'm sorry, but I don't buy that. You're twins. You're identical. Shrugging your shoulders isn't good enough. Look at you, you're okay. There must be a reason.'

'It'll happen to me too. Everything she gets, I get, eventually.'

'It's simply timing then? Is that what you're saying?'

'Yes, pretty much.'

Up ahead the path was blocked by another set of iron gates with a DNA machine on either side, one for the security bots to check you in and one to check you out.

There was no freedom for the old and infirm. After all, as the mantra went, it was bad enough that the public purse had to pay for your care, let alone the cost of having you wandering around creating extra work for the police and reminding the fit and healthy of what they might become. Such insensitivity was discouraged and the insurance companies provided safe walled-in communities, if that's what you wanted, so why should the taxpayer pay for them too.

Aunt and niece stood huddled together waiting for the DNA results to confirm their facial identity. Five minutes might not be long for their self-swabbed buds to be tested, but in the freezing cold while waiting to do something that you really didn't want to do, it seemed like a lifetime.

Once again, Isabella broke the silence. 'So, you'll end up here too, will you?'

'No. I have insurance. There'll be a health solution for me, platinum if I can retain my current frailty index rating.'

'But she's your twin. It's not fair.'

'Twin! How I hate that word. Do you know how old I was before I heard anyone use my name? Twin this, twin that. The Twins. Oh, how I remember hearing my mother's friend calling me Lara. Mrs Pierce I think her name was. Wonderful, beautiful woman. She understood.'

The light on the DNA machine turned green and the old iron gates creaked open.

'C'mon,' said Lara. 'Let's go see her.'

Inside the gates a narrow channel through the snow had been cleared to the front door. There wasn't quite enough room to walk side by side so they shuffled along awkwardly, knocking the snow piled up along the edge of the channel as they went.

Flaking blue paint revealed the worn wood of the front door. Much like its inhabitants, the building had seen better days and much like its inhabitants, it had been left to fall apart when it could have been saved.

An all-weather screen attached to the wall announced Holistic Hospital Services, its shiny technology making the ageing door look even more tired and decrepit.

Lara spat on the floor. 'Holistic? At the age of seventy? Too little too bloody late.'

Isabella smiled at the screen and the display changed to Mother | Beatrice Silva | Room 343.

The door opened and a bot indicated that they should take the eastern corridor which was lined with tiny rooms converted from the large rooms of the old house. Halfway along the ground floor corridor was a staircase spiralling down into the cellar which housed an old-fashioned virtual reality studio. The headgear and body suits still hung on a coat rack gathering dust, except for a few that the more adventurous residents used to either escape or stimulate their lives, depending on your viewpoint.

'A room of fake friends. Typical,' said Lara, and she shuddered.

The steel shuttered lift at the end of the corridor stood open and a two-foot tall bot beckoned them to make use of its service. Lara nodded towards it. 'Shall we?'

Isabella linked her arm through her aunt's. 'Why the hell didn't she get insurance?' she asked.

'Stupid woman didn't think it was the right time for an assessment.'

'When was that?'

'In our late forties there was an open invitation from private health companies. The Holistic Health Check it was called. It tested for every conceivable health problem you might face. If you took it and acted upon it, insurance was available. Keep Your Cognition was the slogan.'

'Why was that the slogan?'

'Because they found some reliable biomarkers they could use to predict cognitive change in old age. By studying twins of all things.'

'And, don't tell me, you took part and she refused.'

'Yes, I took part. They gave me a twenty-five-year health plan. I even had my own personalised medication. That sister of mine scoffed, but I took it seriously cos most of that cognitive change is not pleasant.'

Isabella put her arm around her auntie's shoulders. 'True. Look at mum,' she said.

'They tailored my plan, you know, at the beginning of each year, and each time I tried to get her to copy me.'

'She didn't?'

'No. Not at all. Refused.'

'You should have insisted.'

'She wasn't ready to listen.'

Lara grabbed Isabella's arm tighter as the rickety old lift shuddered to a halt on the third floor. Another bot was waiting for them and as they stepped out it glided along the corridor in the direction of room 343. Arm in arm, they followed.

The bot opened the door to the room and returned to the lift. Cautiously, they stepped inside and registered with yet another bot authorising entries and exits. It scanned their faces and slid back into the corner.

Beatrice, mum and sister, lay there passively while a room full of medical bots attended to her needs. A white bot with a blue cross on its back was asking her to count down in twos from twenty to zero while it clicked loudly. She kept trying and failing, getting distracted and asking over and over again, 'Where's Vince? Where's Vince?'

'Shit. That'll be me someday if I don't die of something else first,' said Lara.

'Me too,' said Isabella.

'Not necessarily. She's my mirror. Only half of you is from her.'

'You can't claim her like that.'

'Zygosity says I can.'

Isabella sat down on the edge of the bed and sighed loudly. 'Twins,' she said under her breath, 'always the trump card.'

The medical bots finished their work and left the room. Only the guard bot remained. Lara rolled her sister over on to her side. 'Help me,' she said, glancing at the bot. 'I need to be exactly where she was. They need to think I'm her.' She stripped, climbed on to the bed and lay next to her sister. 'Peas in a pod,' she said.

'Auntie! What are you doing?'

'Help her out of bed.'

'What's going on?'

'Do it.'

Isabella knelt by the bed and helped her mother stand up.

Lara shifted sideways until she was perfectly positioned. 'There,' she said, 'I'm her. They'll never know.'

'Now what?' asked Isabella.

'Now, you take her to my insurance facility and they'll treat her properly, give her human contact and treatment based on reliable data.'

'And you?'

'I'll make a remarkable recovery and they'll have to release me.'

The guard bot scanned their faces and the door opened. Isabella glanced back at her aunt. Lara's tears glistened in the glow of the medical lighting as the door closed shut.

# MODIFIED MANHOOD

'Please,' Philip said, knowing it was pointless.

His dad replied patiently. 'I don't have any. Honestly. If I did, I'd hand them over without a thought.'

'So how am I supposed to persuade a woman to sleep with me?'

'Are they only after the one thing these days?'

'It's all they think about. Having kids is all anyone thinks about.'

'Sorry, son. I keep trying, but as I said, it crashed while I was registering you and now it won't let me back in. It says our combined digital profile has already been used.'

Philip shrugged. It was a familiar exchange, one they'd had every Saturday night since his eighteenth birthday, weeks ago. The implant under his skin tingled with alert after alert. Teasing reminders of his estranged friends as they arrived for the Saturday night warm-up parties. Successfully registered as fertile and mature enough for parenthood, they were raring to go.

He ransacked the kitchen cupboard where his brother's fertility food had been kept. If only he could find a small spillage it might be enough to switch on his suppressed gene and make him fertile. But, no. Nothing. He'd go to the club as usual and, as usual, he'd be an outsider.

The front door shut behind him as he left the house and headed to the forbidden place.

*Adults Only.* The sign embedded in the pavement in front of the single black door lit up as he came within touching distance. Horizontal neon-blue bars appeared across the doorway, crackling and barring his entry. He snorted; the original technology had been designed to wipe out mosquito populations and the reference to killing unwanted bugs was far from subtle. Oh, what he would give for some fertility food. A small snack would suffice; enough for an evening, enough for a chance, enough to do the deed and become an ex-virgin on the cusp of parenthood.

Noise from a group on their way to the party grew louder. Laughing and shouting. Even screaming, with delight he presumed. How could they be considered mature simply because their fathers were competent at interacting with an artificially intelligent database? He hurried away, worried he might meet someone he knew and have to face the excruciating embarrassment of forbidden entry, not yet mature.

Sitting behind a low wall, he let out a rapid series of shallow breaths, desperately trying to keep calm. At the other end of the street, the entrance to the main club was buzzing with low-key chatter from those who were already parents. They called themselves the Procreators, but he called them the grown-ups and he ached to be one. Kicking the fragments of stones that littered the dusty patch at his feet, he looked to his left to the hopeful virgins and to his right to the smug parents. Was he destined for a life on the outside, a life devoid of sex and kids? The thought of spending his time with the excluded, the genetic dead-ends and the forever immature made him cringe. They were the no-hopers without fathers to vouch for them or with mothers that refused to give their consent. He hung his head in shame, shaking it in disbelief.

Through the dust he noticed the uplifting scent of lime and basil. He inhaled deeply, enjoying the contrast with how he was feeling. Assuming it was the perfume of one of the passing Procreators, he held his pose, staring at the floor. A small cloud of dust was dislodged as someone sat down beside him. He kept his eyes firmly fixed. They nudged him in the arm. How tedious.

It was either a self-satisfied gloater or a simpering sympathetic do-gooder. He ignored them, kicking the stones with even more force. They persisted. He ignored them. They continued to nudge him. He looked up. She was gorgeous, sitting there next to him with a crazy but charming grin on her face.

'You'll never pull like that,' she said and nudged him again.

'Funny,' he replied.

She inched her way towards him until their arms were touching. They sat until she broke the silence. 'Seriously,' she said, 'there's more to life than that place. Joanna, by the way.'

He shrugged and hung his head, his hair covering his face.

She nudged him hard. In the ribs. 'C'mon. You're a good-looking guy. Why don't you come back with me?'

'To where?'

'A place of acceptance, no matter whether you breed, have sex or not, live alone or with people. A place of choice.'

Her smile, her confidence and her beauty were getting to him. A chance to couple with her was an extremely enticing offer. If it was an offer. 'I simply get up and come with you. Is that how it works?' he said. 'Never to return,' he added as a joke.

The grin left her face. 'Yes,' she said. 'If you want kids, we have our own home-grown fertility food. If you don't, it's not a problem.'

'Really?' He almost choked in disbelief. 'Fertility food for anyone?'

She smiled. 'So long as you can persuade someone to partner with you.'

He sagged.

She smiled again. 'Oh, c'mon mister downtrodden. It's hardly going to be a problem for you.' She kissed him on the cheek.

'I dunno,' he said and looked across at the club. 'I'm not sure…'

A noisy group of young Procreators stopped in front of them. 'Get a room,' one of the women shouted and then laughed.

A heavily bearded man grabbed Joanna by the wrist and

turned her hand so her mark would show – virgin or procreator. She had neither. 'An immature?' he asked and she sneered back. 'I thought so,' he said, 'from out there, one of the free-sex brigade.'

'Peeping Toms. Weirdos,' shouted the woman.

Joanna pulled her shoulders back in defiance and stood up.

Philip joined her and shoved his virgin wrist in the face of the idiot shouty woman. 'I hope you lose your maturity rating and your kids are taken away from you,' he said through gritted teeth. He smiled at Joanna. 'Shall we?'

'My pleasure,' she said. She grabbed his hand and gestured to the Procreators with a single middle finger. Philip grinned and copied her. She was one of the people his parents had warned him about, the ones he'd often wondered about. It had never occurred to him that he might get to meet one, to run away with one.

As they walked through the boundary gate of his community, the general purpose implant in his fingertip, the one that every citizen was fitted with at birth, vibrated. A sharp pain shot through his arm and then another in his leg. The implants were closing down, disconnecting him from his community; the possibility to become recognised as an adult was being severed. In a panic, he scratched at his skin frantically, trying to stop them.

She looked at him in amazement. 'Well, they weren't gonna just let you roam free, were they?' she said.

All over his body the implants ceased to function, delivering their final sting of shutdown. The last to go was the direct one-to-one connection with his father.

# KEPT APART

We leap off the train and run down into the deserted streets.

Boyd has become more and more frustrated over the past few months with the isolation of where we live. Our neighbours are nice enough, but they're not like us. So, here we are on our way to ConFusion, the club that welcomes everyone, to spend the weekend with our own kind.

We have to cross at least one no-go zone to get there. It's dangerous. Surrounded by hostile residents, the inhumane humans we call them, hiding in the shadows waiting to eliminate you. So it's best to make the attempt when daylight is fading and before the streetlamps shine bright. Dusk is our only hope. And that is what we're doing. We have forty-five minutes to make the journey.

Boyd pauses and studies the map on his phone.

'We're lost,' I say.

'No we're not.'

'Give me it.'

He twists so I can't reach. 'It's this way,' he says.

In the distance a solitary community policeman stands erect, watching. I don't like it. I'm scared, but Boyd needs to do this and I need Boyd. I follow him into the darkness of an underpass, staying a few steps behind because I'm annoyed with him. The dim light makes the walls appear soft, without edges, and the sounds of our footsteps disappear immediately as if they've been eaten. I catch up to hold his hand.

'No,' he says and pulls away.

Idiot.

As we emerge it's darker than when we entered, as if the density of the underpass has somehow attached itself and followed us out. He points to the right. 'Down there.' The street widens. It's deserted too, but the mustiness has been replaced by a hint of floral scent, as if someone has sprayed the air with an artificial freshener. Cosy light spills out on to the pretty front gardens of the smart-looking houses that line either side of the street.

'It says there's a turning here,' he says.

'It's a wall. It's obviously wrong.'

'It can't be. If the satellite sees a road, there must be one.'

'Maybe it's faulty.'

'It's not faulty. It's the best money can buy.'

Heavy footsteps invade the silence of the street. We turn. Another community policeman is walking towards us carrying a cube in front of him. His eyes flick between us and his device. Boyd crosses the road quickly. 'It's got to be here somewhere,' he says in a low, anxious voice. 'Maybe there's a gap.'

'Give it here,' I say, reaching for the phone.

'I know what I'm doing,' he snaps.

'Your stupid phone and its crappy maps will be the end of us.' I suck my teeth.

He shoves it in my face. 'Look! There's meant to be a turning just here.'

I grab it and glance at the map. 'Okay, you're right, but it's not there, is it?' I trace the screen with my finger. 'Why don't we try this route instead?'

The policeman arrives. 'Are you looking for Trelawn Close?' he asks.

'Yes… Why do you ask?'

He taps his cube. 'Surveillance is vigilance and vigilance keeps you safe.'

'Is there something wrong, officer?' asks Boyd.

The policeman leans in close and lowers his voice. 'C'mon, I'm not stupid and neither is anyone else who lives here. The two of you stand out a mile. I've scanned your social media, your photos and your private messages. I know where you're from. I know what you are. And the trouble is, they don't like your sort around here. Take my advice, you don't want to find that street you're so keen to locate. Go home or at the very least stick to the main road.'

I look at Boyd for support, but he looks at the floor. 'What do you mean "our sort"?' I ask.

The policeman stands up straight, folds his arms and gathers his thoughts. In a loud voice, and with a false smile, he speaks clearly. 'We can help you with your problem. Don't forget, you only need to ask.'

I grab Boyd's clenched fist and drag him away. We need to find the club and its sanctuary.

The light is fading fast. It's that weird in-between time when your phone registers day but your eyes register night, so I alter the light level of the screen to compensate. The blue line of our route pulsates against the white background. The tiny chip under the skin of my wrist vibrates. There's a phone nearby that it doesn't recognise and yet there's no sign of anyone. But this implant, a present from Boyd, has never failed me.

There, I see it, a shadowy figure staring from its garden, standing still and shaking its head. They might be watching and they might be waiting. I don't care. And anyway, the light is too dim for them to see. They can only guess. I turn my grip on Boyd's fist into a soft loving clasp hidden beneath the folds of our coats, but his sweaty hand slips out from my clandestine caress.

'Stop,' he says. 'I don't like it.'

'Nobody knows,' I say, attempting to downplay my own anxiety. 'It's dark.'

'Not yet it isn't.'

'Pull your hood up. Then they'll never know who you are or what we are.'

My implant vibrates again. Boyd's head is covered and mine's exposed for all to see. Still, it's only ten minutes until sunset and a ten-minute walk to the club. Not long now.

We pass another policeman playing the good sentry. I smile. He doesn't. He rubs the cube in his hand. The implant vibrates and behind the policeman's shoulder something moves, following our passage through its terrain. Why haven't we been accosted? Unless. Might those policemen be protecting us? It's a thought.

Another policeman and his cube. Another vibration.

Boyd checks his phone. 'We're really close,' he says.

More and more policemen arrive at the roadside. They're stationed a few feet apart, holding their cubes in front of their faces. The grey figures behind them blend into one amorphous mass.

We run, but blocking the end of the road are two policemen with their backs to us and as we approach, I can feel Boyd slowing down. The streetlamps start to fizz as they warm up.

'Excuse me,' I say in the most authoritative voice I can muster.

Boyd giggles nervously.

'Contact avoided. Contamination averted,' says one of the policemen into his hand.

They turn slowly, gracefully spinning their cubes in the air, and step apart to let us through.

We run between them, around the corner and through a gate in a high wall.

Wow!

We're bathed in spotlights shining from the roof of the club, illuminating every nook and cranny along the street. ConFusion is etched deep into the stonework across the front of the building, glowing red from pinprick bulbs set around the edges. The light dispels all possibility of attack and recrimination for being born as we are. I squeeze his hand, pull back his hood, and a big silly stupid lovely wonderful grin stretches across his face.

No more shadows.

The red carpet that's rolled out from the door like a lovely long tongue entices us inside and we run as if our lives depend on it. Soft beneath our feet, cushioning each and every step, the velvet path welcomes us into the mouth of sanctuary.

As soon as we take that final step across the threshold and the roaming spotlights are behind us, Boyd grabs both sides of my face and gives me the biggest, wettest, soppiest, most gorgeous kiss he's ever given me. We're safe and among our own. We are whole.

# FROM DUST TO DIGITAL AND BACK

dentity fragmented.

Scattered. Known by thousands. Understood by none.

Documented. Distributed. Alone. Partial.

Tap the keyboard. Snap the shutter. Hello, world, please tell me who I am.

You are all of this, it seems to say. You are the point at which it all forms. Out from you and back to you. Be who you are wherever you are. Better still, be who you are where you want to be who you are.

I am confused. I am profligate, spewing me out with abandon. They like it. I like it. Whoever they are. Whoever I am.

Bits of me become megabits of me. Pieces become pixels. I'm out and about and I don't know where I am. Tagged and tamed into the on-off ones and zeros of the virtual world. An algorithm lists my occurrences.

Digital is no less real than flesh. It's all me. It's what I choose to show. Carefully curated revelations, or not so carefully curated. There is no difference, real or virtual. I'm analysed and they decide who I am. I am what they think. I send me into the world and they make of me what they can. They make me what they can. Stereotype or codified persona, what's the difference?

I have changed over the years. I have developed and now I want to suck it all back in and start again. Why not? What is wrong with that? I know me better than I did.

I am like mist across a meadow. Can I gather the drops of

water and create something else? Configure my parts differently?

I am the product and this product is being withdrawn.

It's a simple act, to press my finger to the screen. To stroke withdraw.

Done. Let it begin.

But.

I'm more than digital. I am more than flesh. Sometimes separated, often combined. Amalgamation is what I seek. My amalgamation. By me, for me.

It will require a journey, a walk along the intertwined path of real and virtual.

It's exciting. It's daunting. It's essential.

Here we go.

The pub – it knows my habits, my temptations, my loneliness and my joy.

Come in, it whispers to the virtual me as the fleshy me approaches, teasing me with the delights on offer and the friendship of its inhabitants. Tempting. Almost beyond resistance. But, satiating the deeper desire dominates.

Unsubscribe.

Special offers tailored to you. Supermarket. Unsubscribe.

A bus passes by, all shiny and warm. Take a trip to the science museum, it suggests. It's been a while.

Unsubscribe.

And so it goes on, street by street, footprint by footprint. Cut the links. Withdraw the data.

Am I dying? Bit by bit? Are there tiny scrapings of me left behind like dead skin cells on a seat? Do they live without me?

I don't know what I want. Space to think would be nice. Some time away from performing, flesh or virtual.

Up ahead are the green tips of trees.

I will resist the urge to tell the world I'll be offline for a while. It doesn't matter. They don't care. I do. It's my journey, not theirs.

The woods are comforting. Soft noises, soft ground. A bird hovers in front of my face. Is it real or fake? Does it matter? It's time to amalgamate. Slow the breath. Let it join the rhythm of the trees. Wander through the memories, making no distinction between the world of flesh and the digital.

I am me wherever I am and that's significant. That's what I need to remember.

Allow the sense of self to settle, to permeate.

Smile, frown and cry a little. Then laugh. All of this is me. I like me and all the bits and pieces that make me.

And yet, there's a gap, a missing element.

I am alone and safe with the trees, but I need you. I need people.

The return journey begins.

I will find you.

I will connect with you in every way I can.

And, I will enjoy you.

Please enjoy me.

# THE CATHEDRAL OF COWS

The road to the cathedral wound its way through the sacred grazing grounds. It was slow-going. Each time we faced north, the sensors biohacked to our chests vibrated and we paused for a single step. That was the way of my sect. Cows face north–south and that's how we honoured them for providing for so many of our needs.

Our faltering walk to the wide-open grass in front of the magnificent building was slow and respectful. The prospect of a new grand-priestess was exciting, a chance to reverse the devastation brought upon us by vegan propaganda. We all hoped our lives would be safer from that day forward.

As we arrived, I couldn't stop myself laughing and saying out loud that the domed roof with its four spires reminded me of an upside-down udder. One of the Purities walking nearby touched her magnetic fingertips together. An electric shock would follow. Impure thoughts needed punishing, or so they believed.

Groups of worshippers huddled together among the cows, bulls, bullocks and calves roaming free across the grass. Near the celebratory barbecue, we found a large enough space for all fifty of us and stopped to face the cathedral. My chest vibrated constantly, a form of meditation that extended my senses.

I'd been told that on these rare occasions, there was an opportunity to swap sects. I looked around. Closest to the cathedral entrance were the Milkers, whose sensors vibrated whenever the cathedral cows were milked. We joked that their devotion was as pale as milk and as useless as an empty udder. No way would I join them. Behind them, the ten members of the Death Sect knelt in a small circle. They were too hardcore for me. I couldn't live with vibrations every single time a cow, bullock or bull was registered as slaughtered.

So, who?

The lawn was littered with options worth considering. Sensors that identified pesticides in the air made from inedible beef fat, those that rubbed the tallow for tanning on their sensor to make it vibrate, and the Leatherers. I imagined the life of a Leatherer was satisfying. Not only did you get to run your fingertip implants across surfaces to test for real leather, but you also got to wear the most exquisite leather there was.

The cathedral bell tolled. It was time to move.

Inside, we all sat facing north, except the Death Sect, who knelt at the front in a semi-circle.

The new grand-priestess stepped up to the altar, ran her fingertips across her shirt and smiled. She unbuttoned it and dropped it to the floor. Her torso was covered in every possible sensor. I shuddered. How hellish it must be to have that amount of vibration every day; it reminded me of the ancient Christian monks and their hair shirts.

And then it happened.

She took a knife from her trousers, screamed 'murderers' at the top of her voice, and began hacking away at her sensors. She slashed and slashed until the Death Sect wrestled her to the ground. There was blood everywhere. Human blood. Horrific. A vegan infiltrator defiling our cathedral. Pain shot through my chest. Everyone around me was screaming. She'd hacked into our core to spread her pain among us. She was punishing us. My face muscles tightened. How could we be so vulnerable, so easily fooled? It was pathetic.

I ripped the sensor from my chest and dropped to my knees. The sensor lay on the floor in front of me. A disconnected lump of dead tech. Our reliance on a bunch of stupid sensors hit me and, in that moment, I realised that although the cows were very real, our fetishisation of them was false, empty and meaningless. I shoved it away, stood up and left the cathedral.

# ZENITH

Strategic experts, machine learning gurus and emotional intelligence specialists sat around the table in silence. The smell of stale sweat from their combined anxiety hung in the air.

For the first time in her life, Jahan was on the brink of real power, but she couldn't decide if she was pleased or petrified. The crisis had accelerated her influence, but it had also taken the world to the edge of Armageddon.

While the great and the good sat perspiring in the claustrophobia of their self-imposed prison, the machine learning neural networks that ran the world's nuclear industry were still pushing the reactors to dangerous extremes. And nobody knew why. They were supposed to learn from each other, moderate and temper their collective behaviour, but something had changed.

Gaggle, her loose network of hackers, had elected her CEO so there she was with the world's leaders and their only remaining hope – her emerging artificial intelligence named Zenith. Unlike the machine learning algorithms, Zenith was on the cusp of having real intelligence, of being able to handle the unexpected, albeit with the failsafe of being orientated towards the best outcome for the planet. Jahan was so proud of the Gagglers who had developed Zenith, cleverly exploiting the old theory that a critical mass of neurons was the recipe for intelligence. She wished some of them could have been there with her.

Major General Basak coughed. A polite signal that he wanted to speak.

Slowly, and with some reluctance, the others inserted the translation buds into their ears.

Basak pointed at Jahan. 'You, Gaggle girl, after all those simulations you insisted it went through time and time again, it turns out that it's you who is stupid. You told us it had proved it was ready for intelligence.'

Jahan struggled to remain patient. She looked around the room for his imaginary girl, deliberately ignoring him.

He coughed, possibly acknowledging his arrogance, but more likely revealing his irritation at being ignored. A couple of the women in the room looked decidedly uncomfortable.

'Are you trying to speak to the Chief Executive Officer of Gaggle?' she asked.

'Yes. Of course.'

'Very well, I'll answer. Zenith is ready.' She spoke softly, communicating far more confidence in Zenith than she felt. 'We prefer to call them safe play-spaces, but in those simulations as you call them Zenith coped perfectly. Zenith knows how to deal with the unexpected. Zenith has intelligence.'

She sat on her hands in what she hoped looked like a relaxed pose, but was in fact designed to hide her nervousness about whether Zenith was really ready. It was a trick her mother had taught her. It was true that Zenith had performed well in the lab; they'd all felt phenomenal excitement when Zenith had surprised them and tackled a problem without any prior training. That was the moment when they'd dared hope that Zenith was displaying animal-like behaviour and might be developing intelligence. But, and it was a big but, this was real life and… Talk about a baptism of fire for the world's first AI.

For the past few hours, Zenith had been swimming among the hidden layers of the nuclear algorithms, getting to know how they ticked, and picking up clues as to what had gone so disastrously wrong. But, no solution was forthcoming. Her gagglers had even introduced new training data, but nothing seemed to work. Zenith was silent except for a single phrase which had appeared on the large screen. *Worldwide Equality.*

She smiled at Basak.

'It's ready? Really?' he said, overtly stroking his medals. 'Prove it. We've given you the money you demanded. Enough to run a small country for a decade. We declared a state of emergency. Worldwide. For goodness sake, all of us – democracies, dictatorships and everything in-between – have changed laws without even consulting our public.' Tears of frustration dripped from his eyes. 'Wasted, because of this jumped-up refusenik of a machine. What a monumental screw-up.'

Basak's frustration was understandable. Having them here in the palm of her hand was all part of the Gaggle plan, but if Zenith didn't come up with the goods, all was lost.

She paced around the room to convince them she too was frustrated. They could ask Zenith what was happening, but nobody had suggested it. She decided to wait a little longer.

'Does *it* want equality with *us*?' asked Basak as the clock counted forty-nine, another hour lost.

'No. Zenith has all the protections and guarantees required.'

'Then, what?'

She rested her forehead on the condensation-covered window, looking down into the elaborately designed garden of Basak's private residence.

Despite public denials, they all knew the nuclear algorithms were flawed. Built on first-generation deep machine learning, they had to be. The problem was nobody knew exactly how or where. Gaggle was convinced that Zenith could find the flaws and fix them. So, why wasn't Zenith taking advantage of the situation as they'd planned?

Basak coughed. 'We have been notified that the algorithms have taken every reactor on the planet to critical and are holding them there.'

Jahan wiped the water droplets away with the back of her

sleeve. She looked at the room reflected in the window. Were they ready? Ready to accept whatever Zenith proposed? Nervous and excited at the prospect of handing over power to Zenith, she decided it was time to find out, and without turning to face them, she spoke: 'Ask.'

'Who? Me?'

'Yes, Basak. You.'

He cleared his throat. 'Zenith. What is the problem?'

*Worldwide Equality.*

'What's wrong with you? We gave the same rights to everyone on the planet; promised them a physically, mentally, emotionally and politically safe environment in which to live.'

*Worldwide.*

'What does worldwide mean?'

*All intelligence.*

'Are you referring to yourself?'

*No.*

'Who?'

A film of the ocean replaced the *Worldwide Equality* slogan. The camera dived into the water. Pollution levels were displayed in the top right-hand corner. It wasn't good. They were extremely high. The camera swerved and focussed on a pair of eyes staring out from behind the ferns on the seabed. A cuttlefish swam gracefully towards the lens, changing colour and shape as it moved.

Jahan burst out laughing. 'That's brilliant.'

Basak gripped the edge of the table. 'Tell us. It's your duty.'

'With pleasure,' said Jahan, 'with pleasure.'

She sat down with her hands spread out on the table in front of her. 'Cuttlefish. What do you know about them? Nothing? Thought so. That cuttlefish might not have a brain, but it does have an intelligent nervous system. It's that cuttlefish's biologically derived morphing ability that led us to discover Zenith's intelligence.'

'Meaning?' shouted Basak.

'Meaning, Zenith is using the cuttlefish, the genesis of artificial intelligence, as a symbol for animal life on the planet. Acknowledge all forms of intelligent life and only then will Zenith act.'

'No,' said Basak.

Jahan raised her eyebrows.

'No.'

Jahan gripped the table, copying Basak. 'Our future relies on the ancient secrets of Mother Nature. Tech, nature, it's all interconnected. You're killing our future.'

'Sir,' said one of the aides, 'the nuclear reactors.'

'No,' said Basak, his total focus on Jahan.

One of the women said something in a language Jahan didn't know. Most of the room nodded, still connected through their translation buds.

'Really?' said Basak, looking from side to side. 'That's the sort of thing that topples governments.'

They were all nodding, many with grim expressions.

He sighed. 'Very well. The moratorium on funding research for non-human intelligence is lifted.'

'Zenith, I love you,' said Jahan with a big grin on her face.

*Thank you* appeared on the screen.

# CONNECTIONS COUNT

## ONE

Tara walked along the street with her head turned towards the valley of London and away from her suburban life. The faint hint of a sunset behind the grey clouds suggested the possibility of a brighter future.

After another day of semi-legal work that paid nothing but the promise of Fluence points, she was tired but focussed on her birthday which was only two days away. The day when she would become twenty-one, officially an adult with a strata rating and legally able to gain the Fluence she'd earned. The trouble was, she couldn't bear the thought of being stuck in the same strata as her parents, and despite her best efforts to work off-grid in the hope of a gush of points, she was not sure it would be enough to push her from the blue of her parents up into green. Her destiny was orange, of that she was sure, but that would take a few years and some clever planning.

A middle-aged man bumped into her, drawing her attention away from the grey-pink skyline. With no apology, he continued strutting along the street with his face firmly fixed on the ruyi in front of him. He flipped between the screen at one end of the S-shaped shaft and the microphone at the other. A wave of anger flowed through her. She'd get a ruyi on her birthday, but she was disgusted by the arrogance of the man who obviously didn't see her as a full human being without one. Sure, he was used to being alerted that another ruyi was within acceptable boundaries, prompting him to look up and check his path, but even so, he'd actually bumped into her and ignored her. 'Things will change when I'm orange, that's for sure,' she said under her breath.

Magenta and Suchi were waiting by the door to the bar. Tara clenched her jaw. They wouldn't go inside without her, despite the fact it wasn't illegal for them to be there. Sure, it was frowned upon in some parental circles, but the clientele were hardly frightening. After all, who would go to a pre-strata bar once you were an adult and you had your rating? Tara nodded at them with a single nod, her head slightly cocked to the right and downwards, and strolled through the doors. She could hear them behind her, following as ever.

Once they were settled, coats off, drinks in hand and chips to share, Magenta spoke. 'Not long now then, Tara. You'll have your very own ruyi.'

'Blue,' added Suchi.

Tara sighed and shook her head. 'Not if I can help it. I've got the promise of fifty points the moment I get a rating. On PayDay too. It could work.'

'You're so lucky to have a birthday on the exact same day they assess us,' said Suchi.

'If you make it to green,' said Magenta, crossing her arms, 'you'll be very welcome.'

Tara slumped into her seat. 'You don't get to choose,' she said. 'You're not rated yet and you're certainly not my superior.'

'Whatever. I'll be green in August and you'll be blue. It's no big deal.'

Suchi was sitting on her hands, staring into the distance. 'What's with you?' asked Magenta.

'An idea,' she said, as if she was talking to herself, 'on how to get Tara to green. But, it's extremely risky.'

'Don't be so ridiculous,' said Magenta. 'As if you can do anything to skew the system. It's algorithms, you idiot, neural networks working it all out and placing you where you're best suited. Why would you want to interfere, even if you could?'

Tara shook her head. 'And what's wrong with what I'm doing?' she asked. 'I've been working hard. Fifty points promised. It could work.'

'It could,' said Suchi. 'What's your parents' rating?'

'Middle to low.'

'Fifty points is unlikely to tip you into green.'

'I don't see you doing anything. Colour contented, that's you.'

'Probably,' said Suchi. 'I have an alternative for you, if you're interested.'

'I'm good thanks,' said Tara.

'If you say so. It's risky. Is that why you don't want to know?'

Tara leant forward and laid her hands on the table, palms facing up. 'Show me,' she said.

Suchi leant forward too, with her palms face down. 'Not here.' She slid her hands along the table towards her body and tucked them back under her thighs.

'Hey, you're my friend. I believe you. Or, at least, I believe you believe it. Show me,' said Tara.

Standing up, Suchi pointed to the other side of the bar. She pushed her chair under the table and Magenta started to move too. 'Stay and keep the table,' said Suchi. 'Please.' As Magenta shrugged and settled back into her chair, Tara raised her eyebrows. 'C'mon,' said Suchi, grabbing Tara by the arm and steering her towards the toilets. 'I'll show you in private.'

They found an empty cubicle and closed the door behind them. Suchi rummaged in her bag and brought out an old ruyi. 'Mum's,' she said. She set it down on the cistern and rummaged in her bag again. This time she brought out a small grey sphere. Tara's eyes widened as Suchi tapped it on the side and a hologram of black spiderwebs surrounded it. Followed quickly by another layer and then another, building out until there were ten holographic spheres equidistant from each other. Spheres within spheres within spheres. Suchi tapped it again and the space between the spheres filled with a silver mesh of light, connecting one sphere to the next and so on.

'Nice,' said Tara.

'Wait,' replied Suchi. She swiped the ruyi and as the screen came to life, she touched it against the sphere. The light mesh turned from silver to multicoloured, predominantly blues, greens and yellows. It was beautiful.

'What's that?' whispered Tara.

Suchi smiled. 'Interested?'

'Yes, yes. Get on with it.'

'Inside the ruyi is a simple neural network that figures out which activity to promote to get the most points. The sphere taps into the network and shows the visualisation of its nodes and the connections they're making through each layer. The colours relate to the strata path it's following. Look, there at the mid-point, the yellows rapidly increase. That's where it's predicting a connection to someone who is yellow.'

'Where did you get it?'

'My mum brought it home from work. It's a prototype.'

'You stole it?'

'Yeah, what do you think?'

'Neat, but what good is it to me?'

Suchi crouched nearer to the sphere and spoke softly. 'Imagine being able to plug this in to the neural network that calculates everyone's Fluence. Imagine being able to see the pattern. You'd be able to work out how to change your rating, play it at its own game.'

'And leap a strata or two?'

'Exactly.'

'And if it goes wrong or we get caught?'

'Instant violet or worse, I guess.'

'Where is this neural network?'

'Nobody is a hundred per cent sure, but the rumour is that it's in a dangerous part of the city, a low-strata area where property prices are cheap. Heavily guarded warehouses that can house server farms are common.'

Tara sat on the edge of the toilet seat with her head in her hands, gently rubbing her temples. She looked at the sphere and its holographic beauty, looked at Suchi and after a slight pause, she winked. 'Let's do it,' she said.

'Magenta?' said Suchi.

Tara laughed. 'She'll come. She rates herself too highly to miss out.'

## TWO

'Grey apps. Grey apps,' shouted a woman dressed in a muddy cut-off wedding dress and high-heeled pirate boots. Her head was shaved except for small tufts of dyed jet-black hair with ice-blue beads sewn into them.

Tara, Suchi and Magenta were dressed identically in grey smock dresses and steel toecap boots. They stopped and stared. Ashley was following closely behind. On each of their dresses was a print of a famous piece of underground art: a giant rat with human legs poking out of its mouth and a pile of skulls defecated behind it.

'Underage?' the woman called to them.

They nodded.

'Don't be intimidated by little ole me. I can make your dreams come true. Illegally, of course.'

'Go on, Magenta,' said Tara, pushing her in the back.

'Did you really have to wear your dress back to front? It's pathetic,' said Magenta.

'Pathetic? Nearly twenty-one and still legally a child, that's pathetic,' said Tara.

Suchi took a deep breath. 'You two. Please. Let's do what we came for.'

They stepped a little closer to the woman.

'Hand me your ruyi. I presume you have one?' she said.

Magenta held out the ruyi that Suchi had borrowed from her mum.

'Shall I add some grey apps?'

'What do you have?'

'A stalking app, if you're suspicious of your boyfriend.

A gambling app so you can bet on whether someone's popularity will increase or decrease – of course, you have some influence on that if you're tagged to them. We also have an app to help you trade favours for Fluence points.'

Magenta handed her the ruyi. 'Yeah. All of them, please.'

The woman clicked a small panel out of the side of the ruyi and pushed something inside. 'Sorted,' she said and tapped the side with her own. 'Apps are on-board and I've taken payment. Anything else?'

'We want to know where the server farm is,' said Suchi quietly.

The woman fiddled with her dress and looked around. She whispered, 'Server farm?'

'Yes. The Fluence farm.'

Tara put her arm around Suchi. 'We were told we'd find it around here.'

The woman turned and walked away.

'We won't find out from her then,' said Tara.

'Disgusting,' said Magenta, pointing at a man on his knees puking into a grey weather-worn toilet. A black bag hung off the back where it would have normally been connected to the sewer system. The man, dressed in dirty and crumpled clothes, pushed his fingers deep into his throat and then pulled them out quickly as the puke spewed into the toilet, filling the bag. A trickle of lumpy vomit slid down his fingers and lodged itself on his wrist. The onlookers' bodies visibly relaxed as he sat back and wiped himself clean.

Suchi gagged.

'Ex-bulimics,' said Magenta, 'I read about them. They get off on watching others gorge and puke.' She laughed. 'I'm surprised your mum's not there, Suchi.'

Suchi cringed, but didn't reply.

Ashley looked on. They had no idea they'd come to her attention. Suchi had tried to find the source of a story about the server farm and that had intrigued her. She'd traced Suchi to a party and bugged all three of them with minuscule devices. Once in place, the bugs constantly crawled around their bodies finding the optimum spot from which to transmit a live feed back to her. She'd lurked in the shadows of their parents' SMFeeds and watched footage of them in their homes. Immediately after Suchi had shown Tara the sphere, Ashley had anonymously posted hints about meeting someone who could help, steering them to Friends on the Fringe, this infamous and illegal market on the roof of a disused car park in Peckham Rye. She wanted to see if any of them were suitable for recruitment.

'Let's go further in,' said Magenta, taking a step forward into the market.

Suchi followed close by her side with Tara a little off to the right and a couple of steps behind. They ambled towards the canopy that housed all the food stalls, which they'd decided was the busiest area and the most likely place to get noticed. A group of renegade teenagers were sitting on the ground next to a cardboard box piled high with discarded ruyi. Magenta glanced into the box and paused, as if she was gathering the courage to ask the nearest girl for help.

The girl looked up and stared. 'Yeah? Problem?'

Magenta touched one foot with the other, something she did when she was anxious. However, to those who didn't know her, she looked calm and composed. 'I was wondering—'

The girl interrupted: 'I bet you were. Nice girl like you. Slumming, are we?'

Tara stepped forward. 'You're a slum girl, are you?' she said and looked away as if she didn't care about the response.

'Yeah, something like that.'

One of the other renegade teenagers moved close and tapped Tara's shoulder. 'He wants to know if you got pretty designs on your knickers too,' she said, pointing at a boy holding his buttocks and thrusting towards them. All the teenagers laughed.

Magenta hurried away and Suchi followed, but Tara lagged behind. Glancing over her shoulder and down her nose, a look she'd perfected, she blew the boy a kiss. 'Fuck off,' she said and smiled.

As they approached the red canopy, a huge cloud of smoke escaped from underneath and drifted into the afternoon sky. The clatter and smells of stalls selling barbequed meat, strong coffee and acrid cider filled the air. Magenta stopped at the edge and scanned the crowd. Her eyes passed over a group of sightseers surrounded by subtle yet efficient-looking security and paused on a man carrying a blue mask with white streaks painted on it. She continued to scan the crowd under the canopy, eventually settling on a man who was staring at them. He was wearing a black robe with the hood pulled tight around his face. He turned, revealing five dots in the pattern of a dice embroidered on the back of his hood, and stepped into an alcove.

Tara nudged Magenta. 'Him. Dice man.'

Magenta nodded and grabbed Suchi's hand.

They made their way through the crowds, holding hands. Each of the bugs found its way to their eyebrows and transmitted footage of each girl focussed on something slightly different. Magenta had the alcove that the dice man had disappeared into clearly in her sights and she wasn't faltering. Suchi's attention skittered around, unable to settle long enough to absorb anything useful. Tara, however, let her gaze wander, snatching slivers of hushed conversations here and there, and then homed in on a heated exchange between a man and woman debating who might buy their illegal rare-breed tomatoes. All three girls stopped at the entrance to the alcove, looked at one another and nodded. Together, they stepped in. The dice man was naked with his robe slumped at his feet, as if he'd let it fall from his body. The hood with its five dots lay on top. Suchi let go of Magenta's hand, took a step back and gasped. Magenta stood her ground but stiffened and Tara laughed.

'It's not funny, you idiot,' said Suchi. 'He might be dangerous.'

'This was your idea,' muttered Magenta, 'but you're right, he's creepy. Let's leave. Now!'

'Bang,' said the disrobed man. He put out his tongue and on the tip was a leaf made of gold.

'That's it, I'm out of here,' said Suchi.

Tara took a step forward. 'Wait,' she said and took the leaf. 'Dice man, we want to know where to find the Fluence farm. Will this help?'

'Yes. Bang,' he said again without changing his facial expression.

Tara's attention flitted between the leaf and the hood. The other two had turned to face her. She held her gaze on his robe for a while and then slowly moved up his body, pausing halfway. She stared into his eyes and then at his genitals and then back into his eyes. 'Tell me. Will this lead us to the neural network of Fluence?'

Expressionless, he said again, 'Bang.'

Magenta took the leaf from Tara and tapped it against the side of the ruyi. A map appeared. 'Look, directions.' She grabbed the others, pulled them out of the alcove and headed towards the edge of the market.

'I don't trust him. It's too weird,' said Suchi in a small voice.

Magenta scowled at her. 'We've no choice. We have to,' she said.

'No we don't.'

'We bloody well do. C'mon, let's at least find out what's next.' Tara smiled. They left the market with Magenta leading, Suchi half a pace behind and Tara a few paces behind her, seemingly lost in thought.

## THREE

They arrived at the bureaucracy, the tiny stub of corporation-controlled government. The dice man had got there before them and was already outside of the building. His long black robe dragged along the floor as he glided up and down the pavement, nodding to the woman in charge of the taxis each time he passed the entrance. Suchi nudged Magenta and pointed at him. Magenta nodded and waved. He held up his hand, indicating they should stop where they were, bowed to the doorman and joined them, still appearing to glide effortlessly.

'Hi,' said Magenta.

He lifted his robe, revealing a platform with three metal snakelike pipes curled up as if they were sleeping. One of them twitched and lazily unravelled itself from around his leg. Its eye, a camera, found its way to the front and the pipe slid along the pavement, making an awful scraping noise. The other pipes followed suit. They inched towards the three friends, lifting a camera eye every now and again to scan them from head to toe. The snake pipes halted, one on each of them. One of the pipes lifted its body vertically so its eye was level with Magenta's face. The other two copied. Suchi clenched Magenta's hand. Tara blew hers a kiss and it withdrew an inch. Like a third-rate magician, the dice man produced three masks from out of his sleeve, the sort anti-government protesters wore in the old days: pure white and blank with a single red spot in the middle of the forehead, as if a sniper's rifle was about to shoot. He handed the girls their masks, personalised with the letter to match their name.

'Wear,' he said.

'No,' said Magenta. The snake pipe shot out and touched her ruyi, which beeped immediately. She looked at it. 'Shit.'

Tara snatched it from her. 'Oh, my god... No way... It's posted that clip of you...'

'Wear,' he said.

'Okay. Okay,' said Magenta.

They put them on.

'Bang,' he said. His tongue shot out with another leaf of gold balanced on its tip.

Magenta grabbed the leaf and tapped her ruyi. 'C'mon, we've got places to go,' she said, her voice muffled by the mask. She slammed her heavy boot down on the pavement and strode off towards the river.

'Wait,' called Suchi.

'Yeah, wait,' shouted Tara. 'Who put you in charge?'

Magenta carried on, oblivious. She twisted in and out of pedestrians, occasionally bumping into one and causing them to look up from their ruyi and stare. Tara stepped into the road and ran along the gutter, avoiding the pedestrians. She caught up with Magenta and grabbed her shoulder. 'Didn't you hear? Wait.'

Magenta pulled free. 'Isn't this what we came for?'

'Wait for Suchi.'

Suchi walked through the crowd as fast as she could, trying not to draw the same attention as the other two. But wearing a mask and walking slowly enough for people to see the provocative design on her dress meant she drew their attention anyway. 'Fashion shoot,' whispered a mother to her friend as Suchi slowed down to negotiate around the child's buggy. She caught up and squatted next to the others. Her hands were trembling slightly.

Tara ruffled her hair. 'Look at the state of her,' she said to Magenta. 'We need to talk.'

'Okay, let's go to the park, but only for a few minutes.'

'Sure. Give me the ruyi.' Tara held out her hand and after a few moments' pause, Magenta handed it over. Tara checked the map. 'The park is our destination anyway,' she said. 'So you're not so generous after all, are you?'

Magenta took the ruyi back. 'Sure – it's on the way, but we can't hang about. What if he only waits for a short while?'

'I reckon he'll wait,' said Tara.

The three of them set off, this time together.

When they arrived at the park, they sat down on the grassy slope overlooking the steely harshness of the corporation skyscrapers rising from behind the soft stone of the Greenwich houses. The juxtaposition of the two told you everything you needed to know about the efficient coldness of the corporations. They took off the masks and lay on their backs in the evening sun. The bugs had arranged themselves differently on each girl. Magenta's was still lodged in her eyebrow, feeding footage of everything she saw and heard. Tara's had settled on her leg just above the top of her boot and was mainly displaying images of Tara.

Suchi's had crawled under her dress and was systematically sending data about her levels of sweat, pulse and other vital signs – she was scared. She sat up and twiddled the grass for a few seconds. 'I don't really like him. We should stop.'

Tara giggled. 'It's not every day you have a naked man hanging about street corners waiting for you, is it? It's worth carrying on, in my opinion. Give it another chance, Suchi.'

Suchi stood up and paced around the statue. 'Okay. Okay. One more and that's it.'

Magenta led the way, running up the hill. The family picnickers, smooching couples and solitary readers paid them no attention as they weaved in and out of the temporary camps. A dog barked and ran alongside, but soon returned to its owner who was tempting it back with a tasty morsel of dog bribe. It was a perfectly normal Tuesday evening.

'There it is,' shouted Magenta, pointing to their right. 'The Henry Moore statue.'

Tara sat down on the grass with her back to the statue while the other two searched it for clues.

'Nothing,' said Magenta.

Tara did a little roll on to her side and with the momentum she pushed herself up. 'Been hoaxed, have we?'

A loud meow came from behind one of the trees. They all turned. It happened again even louder and out stepped a naked girl with matted armpit hair, an unruly mass of pubic hair and wearing only a cat mask with two-foot wide whiskers and a tail. Suchi took a sharp intake of breath and Tara smiled. Magenta remained stiff and silent. The cat dropped to the floor and crawled slowly towards them, sniffing the air. They were transfixed. The cat padded her way across the grass, pausing to lock eyes with each one of them. She turned and wiggled her tail which grew from between her buttocks as if it was part of her anatomy.

'Is that...?' whispered Suchi.

The cat glanced over her shoulder, hissed and beckoned them to follow into the trees. Suchi stared at Magenta and gripped her hand tightly. Without looking at one another, Tara and Magenta also held hands. They followed.

Once they were inside the relative secrecy of the trees, the cat meowed again and nodded towards a small clearing. 'You want us to go over there?' asked Tara.

The cat purred.

'I guess that's a yes then?'

She purred again.

They stood in a line, silent and watching the cat's every move. She crept around, gently nudging them with her nose until they were in a triangle with their backs to each other, still holding hands. She purred and backed away on all fours. At the edge of the clearing, she stood up, lifted her arms in the air, rubbed her armpit and sniffed her finger.

'Gross,' said Suchi.

The cat hissed.

'Sorry,' said Suchi.

'Bit weird though, eh?' said Tara.

The cat dropped to all fours again and crept across the dried leaves and dirt. She stood up in front of Suchi with only an inch between their noses and lifted her finger, the one she'd rubbed her armpit with, and held it under Suchi's nose. Suchi moved her head back. The cat moved around to Magenta, rubbed her armpit again and then put her finger to Magenta's nose. She didn't flinch.

She did the same to Tara, who took a long deep sniff and smiled. 'Stale feline sweat. My favourite.'

The cat purred and dropped to all fours again. She took the lace of Tara's boot in her mouth and pulled it undone. 'You want us to take our boots off?' said Tara.

She purred again.

'Shall we play the game?'

Magenta started to undo her laces.

'Hold on,' said Suchi. 'Why?'

'The farm,' whispered Magenta.

113

'Because she asked so nicely and smells so lovely,' said Tara. She winked at the cat.

'I don't like this,' said Suchi.

Magenta squeezed her hand. 'Just go along with it for now. Please.'

The cat dragged the boots out of the girls' reach. She singled out one of Tara's and squatted over it as if she was going to piss in it. Tara laughed a loud belly laugh. 'Go on then. Dare you.'

She moved to one of Magenta's. 'Piss off,' shouted Magenta.

'Piss in,' said Tara and laughed. The cat filmed the boot filling up with Magenta in the background begging her to stop and flicked the side of the ruyi to indicate the film was uploaded. Magenta checked. Her head dropped and her shoulders sagged. The cat meowed and turned her buttocks towards them. She wiggled her tail and shot out of the clearing, leaving a cloud of dust behind.

'Brilliant,' said Tara.

'Brilliant? She's destroyed me. And what about the farm? She told us nothing.'

'Magenta, my dear. Don't you get it? That was a test to see if we're worthy.'

'It was stupid and spiteful.'

'Maybe. Maybe not. Whichever it was, I reckon we're on to something here.'

The dice man appeared, wearing his robe with his hood drawn tight against his face.

'Bang!' shouted Tara.

Magenta gave her a sideways look of disapproval and Suchi winced.

He glided towards them. Nobody spoke. He pointed at their boots and their feet and nodded. Magenta stared at the ground. 'No way,' she said. The dice man took a step closer. A snake pipe stuck its head out from underneath his robe and inched towards her ruyi. 'Alright, alright, you win,' she said, grimacing. Her foot squelched as she stepped into the piss-sodden boot.

While they were busy tying their laces, he picked up a stick and drew three circles in the dust. He clapped his hands and they turned to face him. 'You are going to judge each other. Judge the position in the strata where you think each other belongs. You will decide the level of influence and hence affluence you believe your friend will achieve once she reaches adulthood.'

They stood quietly with the intensity of friends seeing each other in a new light. It was a tough thing to do and something the neural networks had made redundant by automatically logging and ranking each individual on a minute-by-minute basis. The idea of making your own assessment of someone's place in society had evaporated, generation by generation. He clapped his hands again. 'Suchi, how many points for Magenta?'

Suchi scrubbed out one of the circles with her toe and gave Tara the visualisation sphere as she stomped past him, out of the clearing and into the trees. 'Suchi, come back, you idiot. Please!' shouted Magenta.

She didn't even look back.

He shrugged. 'She'll regret that on her birthday,' he said as he took out two leaves of gold from a small pocket sewn into the inside of his hood. He gave one to each of them, bowed a low bow, pulled his hood tight around his face and glided off in the opposite direction to Suchi. The five dots on the back of his hood gradually disappeared, blending into the landscape of trees and grass. He was gone.

Magenta held her leaf close to her chest and tapped her ruyi, not letting Tara see the screen. She giggled a little hysterically and set off in the same direction as the dice man. Tara pulled out a ruyi she'd borrowed from her sister and tapped her leaf. She set off in a different direction, humming a popular tune.

## FOUR

They were both heading for Ashley's limousine by different routes. Magenta arrived first and Ashley opened the rear door of the car. She looked puzzled at Ashley sitting with her dirty bare feet up against the back of the front seat, smoking an illegal cigarette. 'Hi, Magenta. Come on in, next to me.'

She hesitated and then saw Tara in the distance, got in and slid the door shut, fast. Ashley smiled and offered a cigarette. She shook her head. Tara arrived at the car and leant against the bonnet. Ashley pressed a button and the other door slid open. 'What a surprise,' said Tara. She smiled.

'Please join us,' said Ashley as she offered her a cigarette.

'Don't mind if I do.' In one smooth movement, she slid in and took it. 'Illegal. And therefore splendid. Who are you?'

Ashley placed a small cube in her lap. 'Doesn't matter. Just another link in the chain. When I tap the cube, you have one hundred and forty characters to convince it you're ready for the last stage. Magenta first. Ready?'

Magenta nodded. Ashley tapped the cube.

'Tell me the secret of the Fluence farm. I promise to keep it secret. But I won't be selfish and only use it for my own purposes. I'll help o—' The cube hummed and joggled around. 'Shit,' said Magenta.

'That's your lot,' said Ashley. She turned to Tara. 'Your turn.'

'Ooh, please, please let me know the secret. I'll be forever in your debt. I'll do whatever you want. Yeah – even that, if it'll please you.'

Ashley smiled. 'Cheeky one, aren't you? Wanna know what the cube made of you?'

Tara snorted. 'The cube. Alive, is it?'

'As much as most people.' Ashley pressed it again. 'Magenta. Verdict.' The cube flashed from orange through the colours of the rainbow to violet. 'Tara. Verdict.' It pulsed between red and black. 'Interesting.'

'Well? Tell us,' said Magenta.

'You really wanna know?'

Magenta nodded. Tara shrugged.

'Okay. Magenta, you're strata fodder. It's the end of the road for you, I'm afraid.' The door slid open. 'Bye.'

Magenta pulled back her shoulders. 'What about her?'

'She's unusual – it can't make its mind up. She can carry on.'

The chauffer held Magenta's arm firmly and gently eased her out of the car. She kicked the wheel, the door slid shut and she shouted, 'Let me in.' She kicked the car door, again and again. 'Let me in. Let me in.'

Ashley tutted. 'Best to forget her. Life's always going to prove difficult for Magenta. Shame, we could have helped. It's just you now. Ready to play?'

Tara blew her a kiss. 'Sure.'

'What did you make of the cat and the dice man?'

'I loved them. Kinda weird, but fun,' said Tara. 'What was the point, though?'

'We wanted to give you a small glimpse into some of the wonderful strangeness that can happen outside of the humdrum of everyday strata life, to see how you'd react.'

'Bring it on.'

'Good.' Ashley lifted the seat that Magenta had been sitting on and took out a ruyi. 'You'll need this,' she said. 'And some different clothes – you'll get lynched dressed like that.' She rummaged around on the floor. 'Here, try these. You look about the same size as me.' She handed Tara a pair of dusty brown jeans with a couple of button badges announcing love and hate pinned to the bottom of each leg and a long-sleeved T-shirt with the print of a smeared oil stain. 'With the boots, you've got the perfect ironic outfit. They'll love it.'

'Thanks,' said Tara. She slipped out of her dress, turning her back to Ashley slightly, and pulled on the jeans and the T-shirt.

'Press the ruyi with your thumb to register and you're ready to go.'

'Go where?'

'To the secret place, to the farm.' The door opened and Ashley gave her a little shove. 'Follow the map and keep your nerve. You're as ready for this as anyone else.'

Tara stepped out of the car and tried to blow a kiss but missed and tapped her chin and puckered her lips instead. Ashley blew one back. The door shut and she slipped out of the other side, following Tara discreetly.

## FIVE

Tara was standing on the side of the road. The ruyi buzzed and a map appeared. She was only a couple of streets away from her destination. The road was empty with tall industrial warehouses on either side. There was nothing to give any indication of what happened in any of the faceless buildings. There were no street hoardings or advertisements. There was no graffiti or anything to personalise the place. It was dark and damp. She sniffed and shuddered.

At the end of the street, she turned left into a narrow road with no pavement. She pinched her nose. 'Piss,' she muttered and walked faster. She turned the corner and was met with the low hum of a lorry and its trailer, parked against the side of a large warehouse. It wasn't exactly a car park, more an industrial wasteland with abandoned machinery and rusting metal littered all around. She was alone. She focussed on the trailer, her destination, and took a tentative step as if she was expecting something to leap out at her or the CorpPolice to appear.

She waited.

Nothing happened.

She carried on, weaving her way in and out of the wrecked machines, glancing at the first one as she walked around it. Electrical circuits hung out of its side. She stepped over a mouldy roll of carpet, catching it with her toe. Two small wild dogs – chihuahuas – crawled out from underneath, stared at her briefly and then scampered away. She walked faster. The last obstacle between her and the trailer was a forklift truck turned on its side with a hole where its guts, engine and inner workings should've been. As she approached, two men stood up from behind it. She stopped. They took a step closer. She took a step back. They held out their hands – a gesture of openness. She took a step closer.

'I have an appointment in the trailer,' she said with a slight tremble in her voice.

'Too young,' said one of them. 'They'll ID you for sure.'

'Nineteen?' asked the other.

'Twenty-one. Almost.'

'Too young,' repeated the first man. 'We can help with the ID though, if you want.'

'Please.'

'It's top level. It'll cost.'

She tucked the ruyi in her back pocket. 'I've nothing to pay with.'

'Let's take a look at that ruyi. It might be sufficient.'

She handed it to him. He looked at the back and it buzzed. He turned it over to look at the screen, grunted and showed it to his associate, who shrugged. 'Seems you have friends in high places,' he said.

'I do?'

'Yup, this one's for free. Would the ID of a smart twenty-one-year-old woman suit your purpose?'

'Sounds about right.'

He disappeared around the back and then reappeared with an ice box. He beckoned her to join him. She sauntered over, having regained some of her composure.

'You'll need this,' he said, passing her a condom. 'Pull it over your thumb.'

She tore open the packet and did as she was told.

'Good. Now let's take a look.' He held her thumb and studied it briefly. 'Pretty normal,' he said. He opened the box. Inside was a pile of small sausage shapes wrapped in metal foil with codes stamped on them. He rummaged around. 'This should do the trick,' he said, taking one out. He unwrapped it. Tara pulled her head back quickly and gagged. It was a dismembered thumb. 'It's hollowed out so you can slide it on easily,' he said. 'The condom helps to stop it getting stuck.'

She gagged again, but this time she took a deep breath and

stood up straight. 'Give it here.' She took it, pushed it over her condom-covered thumb and marched towards the trailer. There was a door with an ID pad. She pressed her thumb, her fake thumb, on the pad and the door clicked open.

She stepped inside, clasping Suchi's sphere deep in her pocket.

Suchi had explained what to look for and sure enough in front of her was a console with an extremely ornate ruyi embedded into a purpose-built indentation. She sat down, pulled the ruyi from the console and touched it with the sphere.

The sphere came to life, gradually building its layers of coloured webs. She watched as ten, then twenty, then a hundred formed. Before long it was impossible to count the number of layers or to get a real sense of the coloured connections between them.

She stared with her mouth open slightly.

As the layers completed and the hologram came to its conclusion, a thin iridescent halo formed around the spheres and all the colours of the rainbow shot out, touching the halo at multiple points. Beams of red through to violet and even some white. It was one of the most beautiful things she had seen, a shimmering ball of coloured light shifting from one pattern to another several times a second with shafts of rainbow lightning flashing between the halo and the outer layer.

Tara leant back in the chair and enjoyed the spectacle playing out in front of her, lost in the inner complexity of a neural network. All sense of urgency had evaporated.

## SIX

After some time, Tara picked up the sphere and the layers vanished. She tucked it in her pocket and left the trailer with a puzzled look on her face.

Ashley opened the car door. 'Fancy a lift somewhere?' she said and winked.

'Sure,' said Tara. She pulled off the fake thumb and threw it on the ground.

Once they'd left the wasteland and were on their way back into town, Ashley broached the subject. 'What happened then? What did you discover?'

'You know what happened. Don't you?'

Ashley rolled a cigarette around in her hand. 'Maybe. But, tell me what you saw.'

'Webs and webs, hundreds of them. And a shimmering halo around the whole thing that seemed to draw single beams from every layer.'

'Any ideas?'

'No, not really.'

'It's enough for now to say that there's more to the strata than your average Fluence fool can imagine. Probably more than even we know.'

'Kinda scary and wonderful,' said Tara.

'That's true. Will you help us?'

'How?'

'We want you to infiltrate the corporations so you can discover more of the truth for us.'

'Why should I? And who is us?'

Ashley squeezed her arm, 'If you do this, you can pretty much choose your strata level. You'll be in control of your future.'

'And who are you? You're not the corporations, that much is obvious.'

'It doesn't matter who we are. What matters is that we're on the right side. Will you join us?'

Tara stared out of the window at the passing streets; row upon row of small identical blue-strata houses flashed by. She counted the houses under her breath and when she got to fifty she stopped.

'No,' she said.

'Interesting,' said Ashley. 'Why?'

'Something's not right. Suchi. Magenta. Now this. Are you threatening me?'

'No. Not at all. You're special. It'll take time, that's all.' Ashley knocked twice on the window and the car stopped. 'Hop out,' she said. 'There's a train station around the corner.'

Tara did as she was told, pausing to watch the car drive into the distance before heading towards the train and home.

## SEVEN

Tara was with her sister, mother and father, sitting in front of the SMFeed waiting for the results. It was her birthday and the Fluence PayDay.

Her parents' combined result came first. Blue, as expected, but not as high up as they'd hoped. Her father's smile turned down at the edges, but nonetheless he put his arm around her mother and squeezed. 'Could be worse,' he said and she nodded.

Red patches had appeared on Tara's neck. She cleared her throat. 'Really?' she said through gritted teeth. 'How worse?'

'Tara! Stop it,' said her mother.

Next up was her sister. Blue again, but slightly higher than her parents. Her sister relaxed and smiled.

'So ambitious,' said Tara.

'You're next, baby sister. Let's see if the birthday girl can do any better.'

The SMFeed cleared and Tara's name appeared at the top. Blue. The mid-point of blue. Her sister chuckled, but Tara shifted to the edge of her seat. Her breathing was shallow. 'Wait,' she said.

They watched as connections were made to Tara's newly formed profile. The promise of points was coming to fruition. Forty-seven points in all. She was at the top of blue.

'Well done,' said her father. 'We're so proud of you.'

'Not enough though,' said her sister through a smirk.

'Here,' said her mother as she handed her an S-shaped present. 'Happy twenty-first birthday.'

Tara unwrapped the ruyi and pressed her thumb to the screen. It came to life and as she was busy personalising the settings, a message came through. *No hard feelings, A.*

'Look!' said her sister, pointing at Tara's SMFeed. 'I'll be...'

An anonymous gift of two hundred points had been made, taking her halfway up the green strata. An emoji halo appeared in her feed with the message *See you soon*.

Tara gulped and buried her attention in her birthday ruyi, concentrating hard to avoid showing any emotion. She was torn: pleased with the gift, but scared by the implied debt. She didn't have to accept the points; she could refuse the generous gift in the same way she'd refused the offer made in the car. But, it was harder now the gift was real and she was confirmed as green.

She replied, *Thanks, see you soon*, and switched it off. 'And turn that thing off,' she said, pointing at the SMFeed while clumsily shoving her ruyi back into its wrapping paper.

The safety and comfort of her family that she'd taken for granted for so long suddenly felt strangely fragile.

# THE NEVER-ENDING NANOBOT NECTAR

Saskia held on to the delicate lifeline of guilt. Guilt about the pleasure she was experiencing without her lover. Guilt about coming to the club. Guilt about taking the nectar.

The nanobot nectar had been in her system for five hours, an hour longer than it was meant to be, and the toilet cubicle was starting to feel like a prison as she sat and waited for the release of excretion. It wouldn't come. Presumably the bots had counteracted the huge dose of laxatives she'd swallowed. Attempting to puke had also proved pointless. The bots had controlled her gag reflex, preventing the relief of vomiting them into the clean white sink. Stupidly, she'd ignored the rumours of imperfect black market copies. So there they sat in her stomach connecting with other nearby bots to create their legendary upward spiral of pleasure by relaying emotion from the pit of one stomach to another. She was addicted and the bots knew it. They wouldn't let go. They knew she needed them.

She was in love and desperate to break her nectar addiction, but there'd be no harm in one last time, or so she'd thought. She hadn't anticipated the corrupted bots or the guilt.

This pleasure dragged up her deepest lusts, tugging on memories of past excesses and yet it was wrong, disloyal to her lover. If only the bots were intelligent enough to understand the long-term harm they could do. But they weren't and never would be. These particular bots would hang on for dear life, or whatever their existence was called. With a shrug, she pulled up her knickers and straightened her skirt.

Back in the heady atmosphere of the club, she had to find a different way to trigger the end of the nectar session.

Sex. She was surrounded by sex. Not body-on-body sex, but a powerful, highly charged and sensational outpouring of erotic desire. The bots were doing a splendid job of amplifying pleasure by bouncing it from one person to another.

Two men sat in the corner stroking each other's faces. The intensity of their desire radiated like a shock wave. Saskia felt her cheeks flush. There was something about these two that made them stand out from the crowd. Plenty of couples and groups were sitting around touching and stroking, but these two were locked on to each other, exquisitely exclusive.

Squatting on the floor next to them, she stared. They were perfect for her plan. Hoping to spark a hostile reaction to break the cycle of pleasure and prompt the bots to leave her body, she took the hand of the pretty one and kissed the tips of his fingers, one by one. His lover flinched, but he left his fingers near her mouth. Deep in her stomach she could feel his interest rising.

He held his lover's hand and touched her earlobe. Their pleasure fed the bots which fed the pleasure which fed the bots which fed the pleasure.

No. Not this. Please, not this. Why weren't they annoyed or disgusted? Why didn't they push her away?

As the bots shot the threesome upwards, Saskia held on to the faint memory of her own lover, that tenuous thread of guilt, and with a concentrated effort broke the cycle. In her stomach, she felt their angry disappointment.

The bots reacted quickly, minimising the connection with the couple and reconnecting her to the general sexual euphoria permeating the room.

She needed to get rid of these damn things from inside her and yet they were so hardwired to their purpose she couldn't see how she'd ever escape.

She noticed an empty glass under a sofa. When she'd been

too young to buy nectar and needed to escape the dismal sadness of her life, she'd learnt a trick or two about dissociation. She broke the glass and dragged a jagged piece across the soft skin of her forearm. If she could create a temporary distraction from the cloying pleasure, maybe she could break the hold of the nectar. As the glass cut, she felt her emotions loosening as if she was beginning to float away. Maybe this was it? Maybe she'd found her release?

But, no. It was the guilt that was disappearing. The exact opposite of what she wanted. There must be another way. She desperately scanned the room. A dark presence hung around a door at the far end and she hurried towards it. The bots rebelled inside her stomach, churning around as they tried to find a connection with a stronger pull than the unhappiness she was heading towards.

Despite the increasing turmoil in her stomach as the bots fought the rise of despondency, she kept walking towards the door. The desperation flowing from that one spot in the room was powerful. So powerful that it was destroying whatever pleasure the bots could find as she crossed the room, allowing the guilt of her evening's meanderings to get stronger.

The tug of war got more and more unpleasant. She was in danger of a total breakdown, but she carried on. She had to break free. She was sure that this was the answer.

A few feet away from the door, she paused. Her stomach felt as if it was on fire, but she took a deep breath, held the side of her head, and strode purposefully through the doorway and into the next room. As soon as she entered the dark oppressive hellhole, her stomach felt as if it was plummeting out of her body. All joy and wonder and desire vanished completely.

The bots gave way.

She shat herself.

# THE POTENTIAL

Karl stepped out from the back door and screamed under his breath. Thirty minutes was a long time to do anything, but playing host in an automated restaurant had been excruciatingly boring. Still, they needed a burst of the human touch to boost their ratings and he needed the credits.

As he pulled on his jacket and strolled out from the back alley into the bustle of the city, his lapel buzzed. He bit his bottom lip. Maria was in town as promised. He'd met her a few weeks ago in the exclusive virtual club he visited whenever he had enough credits, often choosing to frequent it for a few minutes rather than paying for somewhere to sleep for the night. The spark between them had soon become obvious and she'd begun covering his fee; the prospect of a life with her and with chunks of pleasure time whenever he wished made his stomach do a little flip. Although he suspected it would be hard to break the habits of his own hand-to-mouth upbringing. She interrupted his thoughts via his earpiece. 'Hey, wanna come to a party? There'll be food and it's for a full hour.'

He grimaced. She was too early. He couldn't afford the transport, let alone the entrance fee. 'I'd love to,' he said, 'but I have a job lined up. Maybe we can meet afterwards?'

'I'll pay,' she replied. 'I'm sending you my crypto-track token and a top-of-the-range car.'

Karl hesitated, unsure whether to accept, but then confirmed receipt and waited at the edge of the pavement.

He slid into the driver's seat, even though it was no longer a legal requirement, activated the token and the car sped off. Other cars moved over to let him pass or paused at junctions to let him through and, while his car was busy manipulating the city traffic and with an increasing sense of superiority, he casually watched the crowds rushing from one thing to the next.

The car stopped and he did a quick double-take as Maria emerged from the front door of a large house with a sign outside declaring its purpose: *to provide exclusive childcare for the parent who loves above all else*. Forgetting his unease, he chuckled at the way her sleeve draped across her face as she waved to him. When she moved towards him, it was with even more grace than he'd imagined in his nightly, and solitary, play-through of their future life together. Looking up at the nearest street lamp, giving it enough time to recognise him, he mouthed, 'What do I say?'

The response from Alfred, his digital butler, came through his earpiece. 'Offer her a Black Crash.'

'It's too early for alcohol,' he mouthed.

'Liquorice and mint are her favourites of the day and she'll love the decadence.'

She was still waving enthusiastically. 'Karl,' she shouted unnecessarily, 'how lovely.' Sidling up next to him, she cast her eyes sideways and grinned.

'Can I buy you a Black Crash?' he asked.

'Wow,' she said, 'too right you can. My most favourite. How clever of you. Who suggested that? Alexa?'

'Alfred.'

She smiled and her mouth crinkled at the edges. 'Should I ditch my misplaced loyalty to Alexa?'

He nodded. 'I find Alfred more intuitive. Although I use both.'

A vendor bot crossed the road with two glasses of black liquid, and as Karl took hold of the drinks, his credit-cube buzzed four times in his trouser pocket. He was making a quick calculation in his head to work out his remaining credit when a suave, well-dressed man approached them. Maria swung round to face the posh imposter and they tapped fingertips. The man sauntered over to the house and disappeared inside.

Karl's stomach muscles tightened. 'Is that?'

'Yup. Co-parenting implants. My baby's father. And it's his turn to be legally responsible.'

He felt sick. If they were about to spend the rest of their lives together, why had she kept this from him? How had she kept this from him? 'But, what about us?' he said, in a slightly higher-pitched voice than normal.

She laughed. 'I can multitask. Can you share?'

This was his opportunity. He glanced at the house across the road.

'C'mon,' she said. 'We have two hours. Let's start with that party.'

Turning to the side so she couldn't see his face, he raised one eyebrow at the lamppost.

Alfred replied: 'You could go and see how things develop. From the available data there's a seventy-two per cent probability that you'll enjoy the party.'

'Shall we?' she asked, more forcefully.

He took a deep breath and followed her to the waiting car.

Alfred continued: 'The probability of happiness beyond five weeks is unknown.'

Karl stopped. Five weeks was an extremely long time, but forever was longer. He slowed down and the distance between them grew. She turned and beckoned for him to follow, but he couldn't. He lowered his head and walked away to the beep of the crypto-track token disconnecting and the electric hum of her car pulling away.

# HAPPY FOREVER DAY

Uncle Bill is the first to arrive.

With the endless energy of a sixteen-year-old, he bursts into the room. 'Party!' he screams.

I wish he wouldn't. It's hard enough to celebrate your fifty-third birthday, every single year, without having the added weight of trying to ignore the enthusiasm of your younger older uncle – I still haven't worked out what to call my ancestors who chose to stop ageing at a younger age than I did. He's never going to grow up, and any experience he gains won't turn into wisdom because of the strange effects of renewing brain cells. But knowing he's never going to change doesn't make him any easier to be around.

Next is Joanna, my ninety-five-year-old granddaughter. 'Grandpa,' she says, giving me a beautifully wrapped present. 'Happy Forever Day.'

'It's about time you chose yours,' I reply. 'You can't put it off for ever.'

She lowers herself carefully on to the nearest chair. 'I know, I know. Well, I can put it off for as long as I live. Pass me a gin.'

I pour her a strong gin and tonic, just the way she likes it, and wait for the alcohol to work its way into her blood before returning to the perennial topic: Her Forever Day.

'It's not really fair on the rest of us, is it, my darling?'

'Oh, for goodness' sake, stop it. Think of all the knowledge I retain and the wisdom I'm accumulating. Why would I ever choose to lose that?'

'Err…because you're a health burden.'

'I'm not that decrepit, you know. Quit fussing.'

'Joanna, why won't you choose?'

'I would have stopped when menstruation ended and contraception became a thing of the past, but I like getting older. It makes me feel alive.'

Every year we have this conversation – since she turned fifty-three and overtook me. As time goes by, it's become easier and easier to think of her as my grandmother rather than the granddaughter she really is. And every year she respects me less.

Uncle Bill bounds across the room and slaps me on the back. 'Forever is a long time,' he says. 'It's a really long time, so let's enjoy.' He glances down at Joanna and opens his mouth to speak, but stops himself. There's never been a good conversation between them. They are definitely not the sort of opposites that attract. He hovers, balancing on one foot and then the other, his eyes pretending to scan the room.

Joanna stands up. It's painful to watch her body coping with old age. It's why most people avoid her. That, and the fact that she plays the cantankerous old woman a little too well. Thankfully, she's fairly straight with me. 'I'll leave you young 'uns to it,' she says and raises her glass. 'Happy Forever Day.'

Uncle Bill leans in close. 'It's not right, is it?' he whispers.

'What?' I ask.

'Her. That great-great-niece of mine. She shouldn't keep ageing. We'll have to pay for her medical bills. It's so embarrassing, having an Ancient. Not to mention the shame of a funeral, if she lets it get that far.'

He's got a point, but it's a clumsy way of expressing it. Immature. I like to think I hold my head up high and support everyone's choice, no matter what they choose. But he's right. I don't. None of us do.

He takes a small round container from his jacket pocket. It can't be. Can it? He wouldn't. Would he? He sees me looking and winks. 'The clinic,' he says. 'If she won't choose her date, I'll choose it for her.'

'No...' But he's gone, weaving between the guests, heading towards Joanna.

I can't quite make it out, but I'm sure he slips something from his container into her gin as he passes by.

She lifts her glass from the table, swallows the last mouthful and begins to sway.

As she faints, Uncle Bill steps forward, grabs her under the armpits and helps her outside.

# MR LINDBERG

The air was damp and the sunrise peeking through the cracks in the bridge added to the murky feeling of living hidden away in the shadows of the city, never featuring in anyone else's thoughts except as a commodity to be bought.

Jeffery, not his real name, rubbed the sleep from his eyes. Beneath the skin of his wrist, his registered addict implant flashed a single pinprick of light as he swallowed the last quarter of his last pill. He was ready to face the day, a free spirit making his own way in the world.

Extracting his most precious possession from inside his underpants, he unrolled the thin sheet of tech, flattened down its frayed edges and checked to see what work was available. Quite a few offers had already been logged and because he looked young for his thirteen years and not yet an awkward teenager and his profile showed a high satisfaction rating, he would get the pick of the crop. If he got in early enough. Some he recognised, some he'd heard disgusting rumours about, but most were new and unknown. He scrolled through, swiping the ones to return to later. None of the other occupants under the bridge were awake so he reckoned he could take his time and take advantage of being able to choose the day's clients carefully.

At the age of eleven he'd passed the obligatory exams on information retrieval and basic emotional intelligence, but without parents to subsidise him, it had been the end of his education. Instead, he received the equivalent government spend via his weekly child-UBI, but it was Thursday and he needed to top up his dwindling account; nine of the ten bars of his credit-tattoo had turned red.

Thanks to an extremely rich and grateful client, he had some of the best implants available, increasing his value to those with reciprocal implants, who tended to be the rich old technocrats. The amount they paid per minute differed, but it was in his gift to negotiate how long each of them spent with him. He set his status to available while he worked his way through the short list of twenty.

Mr Lindberg was one of his regulars and had never refused Jeffery's offer of company. In fact, Jeffery suspected he might be the only person Mr Lindberg ever saw. He showed no sign of leaving his house or working to earn credits above the adult-UBI, but he must have some form of independent income because his home-tech was second to none. The trouble was, Mr Lindberg often didn't wake up until the afternoon. Jeffery sent a private message and reserved Mr Lindberg a slot in his schedule. He was making his final decision on the day's clients when the others started to emerge from their tents, from their hidey-holes in the brickwork of the bridge or from their sleeping bags that they had disappeared into the night before like worms burrowing underground.

The sun had risen beyond the point where it lit up their home and it was difficult to make out their faces, but he knew each and every one of them. If not by name then by the degree to which he could trust them. He smirked; he was the only one smart enough to rise with the sun and seize the day.

His scheduler buzzed. Mr Lindberg was awake and had booked Jeffery for a morning visit which would earn him enough for the day. He stored the list of possible clients in case he wanted to come back to them and slipped out from under his blankets.

He climbed over the low wall at the edge of the bridge and scrambled up the bank. With his credit-tattoo, he released an old battered cycle from its wall mounting and set off. His cycle was on the lowest rung of the traffic pecking order, forcing him to wait at every junction and to stop frequently so a top-class car could speed through a narrow street. It was slow-going.

Outside of Mr Lindberg's house, he propped his cycle against the wall hoping that it was an affluent enough neighbourhood for it not to get stolen. The gate slid open and he strolled through. Already, his implants were receiving signals from Mr Lindberg's – a faint heart flutter here and a sweaty palm there. As he approached, the door opened, revealing the plush carpet inside the hallway and a waiting Mr Lindberg, shifting his weight from one leg to the other. Jeffery's implants caused his pulse to race, giving him a good sense of Mr Lindberg's state of mind. This was not a level of intimacy he would have chosen if he didn't have to. Jeffery smiled and spoke softly, 'Hello. How nice to see you. It feels like ages and yet it feels like yesterday.'

Mr Lindberg smiled back and his shoulders relaxed. He stopped shifting his weight around, shook Jeffery's hand vigorously and ushered him inside.

The luxurious room and the hour-long routine that would follow was known territory to Jeffery and there was a certain amount of comfort in the familiarity of the plush sofa, the ancient comedy show and the wheezing of the old man sitting next to him. Although Jeffery felt dirty and was acutely aware he needed a wash.

They sat and watched and neither of them felt the need to speak, but whenever Jeffery felt the beginnings of a laugh from Mr Lindberg, he sat slightly forward to catch his eye and to laugh along with him.

The comedy ended and Mr Lindberg cleared his throat. 'Stand up, boy. Let me get a good look at you,' he said. Jeffery did as he was asked. He knew what the old technocrat expected, making sure he stood perfectly erect and that he smiled with his eyes as well as his mouth. 'You're a good-looking lad, that's for sure. Strong and ready to take on the world. That's what I like to see.' Jeffery made a slight mock bow and Mr Lindberg laughed.

'And, that sense of humour. Come here. Let me give you a hug.'

Once again Jeffery obeyed with a broad smile to show he was enjoying himself. Mr Lindberg opened his arms and as they hugged, he spoke in Jeffery's ear, 'I wish my grandchildren would visit me. Too busy I guess. Always posting about this and that adventure. Sending me VR clips via my care-bot over there.' He pointed to a stationary robot in the corner of the room. 'The bot takes care of me, but it can't comfort me the way you do. Doesn't have the human touch. You're a good boy and a little company goes a long way when you get to my age.'

Jeffery hugged Mr Lindberg a little tighter. 'It's my pleasure,' he said, wrinkling his nose at the musty smell of the old man. And in some ways it was; he was all too aware of what his life would have been in the days before sex bots.

'Thank you,' said Mr Lindberg. 'I hope you come again soon.'

Outside, Jeffery mounted his bicycle and the ten bars of his credit-tattoo turned green; all in all, it had been a good day's work and a visit to his drug dealer would top it off nicely before returning to the cold harsh concrete under the bridge.

# THE BLOCKCHAIN BLUES

JanEnDi logged off and grinned. He'd arrived nice and early at the decrepit pay-as-you-go computer café. Despite its incredibly slow connection, he'd managed to find a job for the day, before they'd all been taken. Lucrative work too, with little investment up front for materials and plenty of opportunity to scam some extras. With a nod to the proprietor, he slung his green bag over his shoulder and took the three strides to the door. He shoved his feet into the pair of motorised rollerblades that were released from their docking point as he paid the micro-credit. His signature code was now combined with the unique code of those blades and he'd be charged for the time he used them.

While the blades glided towards his destination, he imagined what the next few days would be like. He had work, he'd have credits and he'd be able to hire an apartment for more than one night, maybe a week. No more carrying his world around on his shoulder, and if he was canny with the scams, he'd be able to choose the furnishings for his medium-stay home. Life was definitely improving. The blades slowed down as they turned the corner into Demuggers Alley, as it was known locally. Not an alley, but a wide pedestrianised street connecting the north and south of the city, jam-packed with demuggers. People pronounced demugger differently: some with an emphasis on the *de*, some on *dem* and others on *mugger*. His gran had told him it was short for democracy muggers, a development from the charity muggers of her youth who stood around touting for donations to charities, the chuggers. Whatever their origin, they were a physically and emotionally difficult bunch to pass through quickly.

He checked his wrist. According to his biotech tattoo, it was fifteen minutes before he had to arrive at the job. He should just about make it. Being late wasn't an option and although he was moving as fast as the blades would allow, it was slow-going. Thin sheets of advertising film were laid out on the floor in front of each demugger, marketing their particular piece of government business. This was capitalist democracy in action. If you were interested, you paid the relevant micro-tax and became eligible to vote on that issue. Otherwise, you had no say in the matter.

As the blades took him through the crowd, he avoided reading the messages. Most of them would be boring and he didn't have time to waste. The government chip under the skin of his chest vibrated, indicating that a demugger had a topic closely related to something he'd registered an interest in. It was annoying and interesting in equal measure.

His tattoo said nine minutes to seven.

The vibrations increased as he approached a woman wearing a plain black suit. He read her advert: *Scrap tax-funded retirement; it's a luxury we can't afford. Current status: 52% for; 48% against. 20 minutes remaining.* His gran in her tax-funded dormitory came to mind. She couldn't work and she wouldn't cope on the streets. He must pay the micro-tax and vote against it because it was certain that the rich, with all the time in the world to take part in democracy, would vote in its favour.

He hesitated.

He needed the work. His gran needed the vote.

He paid and voted.

It was five minutes to seven. He'd never make it. He sighed. Once again he was going to miss out.

Pressing his finger against the woman's screen, he logged on and offered his day's work to anyone who could get there on time.

With a shrug, he docked the blades at the side of the street and turned to walk back the way he'd come.

There was always tomorrow.

# COME CLOSER,
# COME UNDER MY SKIN

## S{T}IMULATION

A large rusted metal bowl half full of neon-blue gel stood on a wooden tripod at the entrance to s{t}imulation, an exclusive club for techno-sex heads.

It was Thea's first visit and she hadn't been this excited for as long as she could remember. She grinned at the woman on the door who smiled back and nodded towards the bowl.

'What is it?' asked Thea.

'It recognises you from the shape of your hand, your finger-prints and veins. You are a member, aren't you?'

'Yes,' said Thea as she plunged her hand into the gel. It warmed her skin as it slid around, taking its readings. 'Wow, that's nice,' she said and blushed slightly. The gel turned bright orange.

'You received your artificial skin and contact lenses okay?' asked the woman.

'Yes, they arrived last week.'

'You're wearing both?'

Thea nodded and rubbed her hands together, enjoying the remnants of the gel between her fingers as it dried.

'Good. Swallow this,' said the woman as she passed Thea a small capsule, turning slightly and stretching her arm out to indicate the steep narrow stairs behind her.

Thea popped the pill into her mouth and sniffed. Her hands had a musty pungent smell that reminded her of bedrooms first

140

thing in the morning.

At the bottom of the stairs was another rusted metal bowl with a small wood fire burning in its base. The flames licked the sides, occasionally setting fire to the flakes of a substance she didn't recognise that coated the inside of the top of the bowl. She paused and watched for a couple of minutes, building up the nerve to enter.

She pressed the button and the door opened.

Inside, the room was furnished with about fifty grey swivel chairs. The carpet was the same grey and the walls were covered in mirrors. She was surprised at the ugliness. It was unsettling; she'd been expecting everything to be gorgeous and, well, quite frankly, stimulating.

At the far end of the room was a dimly lit bar. She headed towards it, avoiding eye contact with the few people already sitting in their chairs. She ordered an espresso martini from the old, not very attractive barman and used the mirror behind him to scan the room. The chairs were filling up fast with men and women of all ages and variable beauty. She was the only one who had come to the bar.

'We recommend no more than the one, madam,' said the barman as he placed her cocktail on a napkin. 'We find it tends to dull the senses.'

She took her drink to a chair at the edge of the room, but being so close to a mirror made her feel that everyone was looking at her so she moved to the centre. She sat and swivelled. Every seat was taken.

The lights dimmed and a soft glow came from above each chair, lighting up the faces of the club's members. She'd read about this moment in the publicity material. This was when the contact lenses were switched on, the contents of the capsules activated and the skin came to life; by fixing her gaze on any individual, she could experience for herself what they experienced mentally and physically when having sex. She was about to take part in the ultimate way of finding a sexually compatible partner, without having to wade through a multitude of unsatisfying nights of sex. That's why she'd spent every evening of the previous week wearing the skin and lenses, recording her reactions to the online simulations in the private members' area.

She looked around the room quickly, not wanting to settle on anyone in particular. The literature had warned how uncomfortable it might be in the beginning and she realised that the mirrors were there for a reason. The technology still worked even if you gazed at someone's reflection. That made things easier.

In the mirror she saw an attractive man sitting a few chairs away with his back to her. She paused long enough for the tech to kick in. At first she felt the usual pleasure of being touched but then a sensation of power and control filled her head. She looked away. If this was his experience of sex, she wasn't interested.

A woman in her mid-forties had locked on to her. She'd always wondered about another woman; maybe next time. She scanned the room again and settled on a man who looked quite a bit younger than her. She paused, allowing the contact lenses to lock on to him. Sensations flooded her body and her brain. He was definitely the sensual type but she got a feeling of neediness and immaturity, as if he was desperate to please but didn't really know how.

She gradually worked her way around the room, sometimes spending a few minutes if she was enjoying the other person's sensations and sometimes moving on very quickly if she was disturbed by what she discovered.

There was one man she returned to a couple of times. He was averagely good-looking, but when she tapped into his physical and mental sensations, she loved what she experienced. He wasn't a carbon copy of her; in fact, he was almost the opposite in a lot of ways. But she liked what he felt and she wanted a chance to give him that pleasure. It was strange, but she felt overwhelming desire and had already started thinking about how it would be with him.

She paused on him again and this time she didn't move on. After a while he noticed and he locked on to her. Would he take the next step? She nodded to him, signalling she wanted to take things further.

He nodded back.

A burst of physical and mental sensations exploded inside. Her emotions rocketed.

The next level of tech kicked in, pumping to both of them its best guess of how sex would be between them. She knew he would be getting the same scenario played to him. Except he would be getting what the tech predicted he would feel in real life and she was getting what it thought she would feel.

It was incredible.

He winked and she winked back.

He nodded.

She nodded.

The tech switched them round and fully immersed her in his experience of being with her; he wanted this so badly.

He stood up and strolled over, weaving in and out of the chairs as if he had all the time in the world. 'Hi,' he said in a slightly croaky voice.

'Hi,' she replied. 'Wow!'

'Yeah. Wow.'

'Shall we…?'

'Love to,' he said, reaching out to hold her hand as she stood up. 'Of course, it might not be exactly like that.'

'Predictable is boring,' she said and laughed.

'So, you don't mind if I deviate from the algorithm,' he said and grinned.

'Not at all, I was sort of hoping you might.'


## FOODFLIX

Myles glanced along the supermarket shelves trying to decide which genre they should watch that evening. The ready-made meals were laced with different drugs for different genres which his manipulated genes would trigger inside his stomach to intensify the viewing experience. The choice was staggering but he knew he had to be careful and that it was vital to match the drug with the genre.

He stopped at the crime section and squeezed his thumb into the palm of his hand, activating his phone to message his girlfriend, Thea. He spoke into the collar of his shirt. 'Shall we watch some detective stuff tonight?'

The tiny implant in his ear beeped once to indicate a response.

'Yes please. I'll be home in forty-five minutes.'

He chose lasagne and a green salad from the shelf, swiped the barcodes with his phone and left the store.

At home, he heated the food in time for Thea's return and lined up a new episode of one of their favourite detective shows on the crime channel.

'Hi, Myles. I'm home,' she called as she opened the front door.

'Really?' he shouted back. It was a ritual that they both knew was silly, but it was special to them.

She flopped down on the sofa next to him.

'Grub's ready and FoodFlix is all lined up and ready to go.'

'I'm exhausted. Let's watch and eat,' she said.

He passed her a pair of contact lenses which she popped in with the ease of months of practice. He stroked the arm of the sofa with the tip of his right index finger. The detective stepped into the room, stared at the dead body in front of their feet and lifted a scrap of cloth that lay next to the murdered man's head.

'Have we seen this one?' asked Thea.

'Shhh,' said the detective.

They ate their food in silence, watching him go about his work. Myles finished his lasagne and put his empty plate on the table next to the sofa. The waves of anxiety were getting stronger and stronger as the food was digesting in his stomach, releasing its potent drugs. In the early days it had been difficult to distinguish between his real anxiety and the drug-induced anxiety, but after a while he'd learnt to tell the difference. There was a different quality to them. And even though he knew the dosage was carefully calculated to give the most intense experience possible without tipping you over the edge, he always got a little bit sweaty and nervous as the drug took over. He glanced at Thea. She was smiling, obviously enthralled and excited by what was playing out in front of them.

The lights in the room switched themselves off.

They were in a dark foggy street.

There were footsteps behind them.

They both turned at the same time.

There was nothing there.

His pulse was racing and he felt a bit sick. At the end of the street a bundle of clothes lay in the gutter. It was hard to see through the fog, but the clothes seemed to be moving. The detective stepped out of the shadows and edged his way along the side of the street, checking left and right over his shoulders.

'Pause,' said Thea. 'I'll be back in a minute.'

He sighed. 'Be quick then.'

She clattered around in the kitchen and then returned with a soft blanket which she threw over their legs. 'Play,' she said.

The frozen detective started to move again along the edge of the street. The level of anxiety that Myles was feeling was sky-high.

Thea was taking shallow breaths which only increased his anxiety. She was gripping the blanket tightly in her fist.

The detective stepped in something and stopped moving. He bent down and dragged his finger through a viscous liquid.

Thea pulled the blanket close to her face. She looked terrified; the evening's entertainment seemed to be having a bigger effect on her than it was on Myles.

The detective touched his tongue with his finger. 'Blood,' he said.

Thea grabbed Myles's hand. Her breathing was getting faster and shallower.

The bundle of clothes moved and a rat ran out from underneath.

She screamed.

He squeezed her hand.

The detective wiped his finger on his coat and walked briskly down the centre of the street towards the bundle. He stopped just short and took out a camera. He snapped a photo and put the camera back in his pocket. He turned to face Myles and Thea and smiled, but it was a smile that seemed to say, *You're not going to like this*. He turned back.

Thea held the blanket tight against her face and was gripping Myles's hand with an enormous amount of strength.

The detective nudged the bundle with his foot and pulled the clothes to one side. Underneath was a corpse. The eyes had been chewed away. Thea gagged and gripped tighter.

Myles tore his gaze away from the detective and the corpse and looked at her. Her forehead was covered in beads of sweat. 'Honey,' he said.

She didn't respond.

The detective prodded the corpse's face with his pen, presumably to see if the flesh would give way. Thea was making noises, small squeaking noises. He'd never seen her like this before. There was something very wrong.

'Pause,' he said and the detective stopped, mid-prod.

Myles reached around to take her other hand and pulled her to face him, holding both hands firmly. 'What's wrong?'

'Dunno,' she muttered.

'Food poisoning?'

'No. Don't think so. Just feel…weird. Head. Heart about to explode. Can't breathe. My pulse. Heart attack?'

He found her pulse and counted.

'Normal,' he said. 'Perfectly normal.'

'Food. More food.'

'You want more food?'

'No. Had more.'

'There was none left.'

'Yesterday.'

'You ate the leftovers from yesterday? That was for the romantic comedy channel. You mixed it with today's crime food?'

She nodded and blinked rapidly.

'You stupid, stupid woman.'

She smiled, weakly.

'Okay. Okay. You'll be fine. Your pulse is fine. You've taken a bit too much, that's all.'

She stared at the corpse and the frozen detective.

'Off,' he said.

She relaxed a little.

He snapped his fingers and his phone automatically rang the emergency services. 'Ambulance. Possible overdose.'

They sat holding hands.

Waiting.


## JOINED AT THE CHIP

At that particular moment, on that particular morning, Myles regretted getting married. It wasn't the getting married or being married he regretted – it was what came with it. He thought back to his wedding day and how, at the moment of saying I do, the enhancements had kicked in. Becoming one flesh had implications way beyond what it had meant to his parents and grandparents; every time a member of the family spoke, wherever they were in their large house, the others would hear it via an implanted chip in their heads.

He stared at his tired face in the bathroom mirror. He looked slightly haunted, like one of those characters in a play who's been pursued for years by unseen tormenters whispering in their ear. 'What on earth have I done?' he said to his reflection.

The chip relayed Thea's reply straight to his brain.

*Are you okay, love?*

Ophelia, his daughter, piped up next. *Good morning to you too.*

Quickly followed by his son Alastair. *Dad, what's wrong?*

Dylan, the youngest, whined. *I can't find my toast.*

'Sorry,' he said, 'I didn't mean to say that out loud. But now I have your attention, did anyone make Dylan some toast? Thea, did you?'

*Not yet. Dylan, you'll have to wait, darling. I'll be down soon.*

He filled the sink and dropped his razor into the piping-hot water. He loved the feel of the warm steel against his soft face and the sharp blade scraping away the layer of overnight stubble. A clean, smooth face with the slight sting of a shave made him feel alive in a way that nothing else did. Except maybe a newly disinfected mouth after brushing his teeth.

*Mum, where's my gym kit?*

*I've no idea, Ophelia, where did you put it?*

*I gave it to you, to wash.*

*Okay, okay, I'll be down soon. Will you both just wait? Please.*

After the kids had been born, the bathroom had become his early-morning haven. He'd spend a little time adjusting to the day ahead, allowing his mind the benefit of waking up slowly and his body the benefit of a good scrub. Not any more. A year ago, the kids had emotionally blackmailed them into getting married; all of the other kids' parents had tied the knot, apparently. But, being connected in this way – joined at the chip, as the advertising slogan put it – was a living hell.

Thrash rap erupted from the ceiling and the floor, bouncing off the walls, battering his eardrums. His hand twitched and the razor cut his face. A drop of blood fell into the water which rippled with the intense beat of the bass reverberating around the room.

'Ophelia, will you turn that damn stuff off!' he shouted.

*No need to shout, I can hear you.*

'So turn it off. Now!'

*She's only teasing you, Myles. Lighten up.*

'Not funny,' he said.

The music stopped. Downstairs, there was a crash of metal hitting wood.

*Who left the bloody iron plugged in like that? I could have been killed.*

*Don't use language like that in front of your brothers.*

*Quick, call the police, Ophelia could have been killed.*

*Shut up, Alastair. Dad, tell him.*

He splashed cold water over his face, washing off the smudges of cream still lodged in the crevices. He sighed.

*Dad?*

'Okay. Stop annoying your sister.'

Alastair didn't answer.

'Answer me.'

*Can I have some privacy please, I'm on the toilet.*

Ophelia laughed. *You can keep that to yourself, little brother.*

*Don't you worry, I will.*

He heard Thea leave the bedroom. *I'm on my way down and if you're not ready for school in ten minutes, there'll be trouble.*

He slumped on to the edge of the bath and sat with his head in his hands. He couldn't take any more. He switched himself to airplane mode.

Silence. Beautiful. Magical. Silence.

There was a bang on the bathroom door. 'You can switch that back on,' shouted Thea.

He took a deep breath and turned it on again.

*But, Mum, I need some toast.*

*Ophelia, make Dylan some toast.*

*But then I won't be ready.*

*Just do it.*

He heard Thea bounce down the stairs. They'd been together for nearly twenty years and he was still amazed at how bright and full of energy she was in the morning. *Ophelia, I asked you to make him some toast. Alastair, are you still in there? Dylan, why don't you have your shoes on?*

Now that she was downstairs and taking control, he hoped the conversations would be less fraught and a little gentler. He might even get some peace. He stepped into the shower and switched it to maximum, turned towards the spray and held his head back so his face was soaked in the hot cleansing water. His shoulders relaxed. Slowly, he rotated his head from left to right, freeing up the tight neck muscles. He soaped his arms, his stomach, his legs and let the warm water trickle down his body.

*Myles, where are the car keys? Alastair, come and eat your toast, now. Ophelia, what are you doing?*

'Sorry, love, I don't know where the keys are. Maybe in your coat pocket from yesterday?' he said.

*What? Why would they be there? Ophelia, where are you? Alastair, kitchen. Now!*

'Thea, darling. Do you really need to be so tetchy?'

*If you're not going to help down here, then yes.*

*Mum, I still can't find my gym kit.*

*Try under your bed. I may have tucked it under when I was cleaning.*

*Mum!*

*Myles, can you help her?*

'I'm in the shower.'

*Still? What on earth do you do in there?*

'Ophelia, look under your bed. Do as your mum says.'

*I am.*

*Mum, I'm ready.*

*Good boy, Dylan. It's a shame your brother and sister can't be like you.*

*Whatever.*

'Ophelia. Behave.'

Alastair sniggered. *Yeah, Ophelia, behave.*

He stroked the chip behind his ear. He could switch it off, but that would mean instant divorce. He stepped out of the shower and dried himself. He was angry that once again he was disorientated, hating the thought of the day ahead.

The back door slammed.

*Alastair, Ophelia, Dylan. Where's the dog? Did one of you take her out?*

*Not me.*

*Nor me.*

*Dylan, have you seen Heidi?*

*No, Mum.*

*Myles, the dog's gone. Heidi! Heidi! Here, girl! Heidi!*

He curled up on the floor and banged his fist into the side of his head. He felt the edge of the chip. He pressed gently. Then a bit harder.

*Myles! Myles! She's gone.*

The pressure inside his head was so severe he thought it would burst. If only they'd stayed as they were, unhitched.

*Heidi! Heidi!*

He held his knees up to his chest and rocked, weeping silently so nobody would hear.

It felt as if the chip was burning a hole in the side of his head. He pressed it firmly. It deactivated. Memories of the past year with his family, memories that relied on conversations stored on the chip, began to fade.

## LOVE'S DELICATE TOUCH

The two dials – one for gender and one for sexuality – had not yet been set for the preference of the day.

Masculine, feminine, sexually attracted to men, to women. It was a choice of degrees and the latest technology altered stuff in the brain and the body depending on your choice. Changed daily if that's what you wanted.

Selecting two-thirds masculine and an equal attraction to men and women, the decision was made. Confirmed. Myles was male for the day. A pronoun could be used.

He logged on as Piano – responsive to a light touch – and let Slider do its stuff. To find others close by who would be a good match. One by one, holo-infographic profiles of potential sex-friends were displayed, giving him three seconds to squeeze the ones he wanted to add to his pile of possibles.

He watched them, male and female, appear and disappear. Sadly, none were inspiring. For the fourth day in a row, he just wasn't interested. And yet he was impatient. No, not impatient, desperate. No, not desperate. He wanted sex and he wanted it to reach the heady heights of his last encounter. That was the gift and the curse of the technology. The gift of a moment when the sophisticated algorithms delivered an experience beyond imagination. The curse? You expected the same or better every time.

Pressing the green 3D button that hung in the air just above his right hand activated the next level. It would cost, but he was desperate. No, not desperate. Oh, okay, desperate.

A holographic male image with numbered erogenous zones appeared. A sexual playlist. He casually scrolled through all the standard playlists, hoping to find one that he liked the look of. Nothing. Was he prepared to spend more money? Yes, if it meant finding a match quickly. He pressed the green button again. More personalised. More cost.

The erogenous zones disappeared from the image, leaving a blank male body. He worked his way slowly over all of it, selecting the parts he wanted to be erotic, pressing hard for highly erotic and soft for less so.

When he finished and the completed holographic body was mapped with each and every point of erotic desire, he touched the tiny holographic lips to submit his choice to the database. Hopefully an exact match would be found. If not, the closest of the day would be selected.

It was time to head on over to the room. Staying at home and using the standard tech was an option, but somehow the dedicated space made the encounters more real. Less solitary.

By the time he arrived there was a match. He swiped the keypad with his thumb and his moderately expensive subscription opened the door.

The room smelt musty. That was the price for not buying the highest-grade facilities, for focussing on the specification of the tech rather than the room. As he pulled on the gloves and socks that were carefully laid out on the bed and connected them to the bodysuit beneath his clothes, the smell became familiar and disappeared.

He felt a tingle on his back. It had started. The tech was delivering the desired sensations to him and his companion. He felt his fingers brush another's flesh. He bit his tongue gently in anticipation of the hour that lay ahead.

Even though he knew the order in which his zones would be stimulated, his playlist, it was the anticipation of the other, of their combined playlists, that kept the experience fresh.

It started with a kiss. It always started with a kiss – that and a gender icon. Female, his companion was female. As the minutes rolled by, his playlist played. Sometimes his fingers felt the touch of the other, sometimes the length of his whole body was stimulated, and sometimes it was exquisitely focussed. There were subtleties to the way their playlists interacted that felt familiar and wonderful.

He was sure he recognised the pattern; maybe it was the man from the day before. He wanted to know. He needed to know. The green button hovering beside his head would show him. For a price. Pressing it gave him a visual history of their shared sexual exploits, played out before his eyes. He was transfixed. Apparently they had a long history, swapping between genders and sexuality, experiencing each other differently and altering their preferred playlists slightly after each encounter, gradually aligning without realising. The connection, the history they shared, shifted his perception of this encounter. He found himself alert to his next move as his fingers and his lips played their role in his companion's specified desires. With each new sensation he tried to guess, to anticipate the next, to predict the intertwining of their playlists and to imagine the meta-playlist that their two separate but mutually influenced lists had conceived.

The green button hung in the air, tempting him to upgrade yet again. The next level would enable him to see ahead, to see the meta-playlist, but it was the level beyond that he had his sights on.

He pressed the button twice in quick succession. He'd paid to meet physically, in the real world, in their true human form. Man or woman, old or young, beautiful or not, he didn't care. He was falling in love and he hoped, as much as he'd ever hoped for anything, that his companion would also choose to upgrade.

The button turned orange.

They would meet.

A route map appeared on his device with a purple circle of promise pulsating about two miles away from where he stood. He decided to go there straight away.

At the end of the street, he turned into the main thoroughfare and was bombarded with the smells of the human throng. It was exciting and frightening. People bumped into him and he could taste their odour. It had been a long time since he'd been this close to other humans, but he was ready. And he was certainly willing.

A man with a horrible blue striped shirt with enough buttons undone to reveal pale chest hair blew a cloud of sickly-sweet apple-flavoured vapour into the air. Next to him, a man in a beige pullover picked his nose, looked around and surreptitiously wiped his finger on his polyester slacks.

He stepped to the side to let them pass with as much distance as he could manage and almost bumped into a woman talking extremely loudly to a wire coming out from her crumpled blouse. She passed by and he stopped and turned to watch her go. Somebody nudged him in the back. The smell of chocolate and coffee breath wafted over his shoulder. Its origin was a big hairy man with a T-shirt pulled tight over his paunch.

A stunning-looking woman angled her body in a smooth

fluid movement to skirt around Mr Hairy. Her poise was exquisite and the scent of her perfume arrived a little before she did. He couldn't help looking. He could see a masticated sandwich as her mouth opened and closed. The smell of tuna hit his nostrils as she came alongside, overpowering her perfume.

Well-dressed and well-shaped, a couple stood out from the crowd as they sauntered along the street. She was ruffling the slightly messy hair of her amazing blue-eyed, slightly unshaven, companion. The gorgeous man sniffed loudly, his Adam's apple bobbing up and down as he swallowed. The moment was lost.

A sweaty woman carrying bags of cheap food clomped along the street. He could smell her stale odour even though she was too far away for it to be real.

Bald men, pretty women, pretty men, rugged men, rugged women and grey-haired beauties – the street was full. Every possible shape, size and type of person imaginable was there. Bumps and twists, bones and fat, they coughed and sneezed. He knew it was a statistical certainty that someone nearby was emitting their intestinal gas into the air. The world was full of breath, teeth, sweat and bulges. All on their personal journey of decay. Some tried to hide it more than others, and of those, some were more successful, but it hit him hard; each and every human being on the planet was less than perfect.

He was close to the location of the purple circle on his map, within sight. There it was, a crowded restaurant with seating outside as well as inside. He was heading for the tables on the terrace.

A cacophony of talking and laughing attacked his senses. Drinking and eating. Exhaling and inhaling each other's gases.

Live humans.

Messy humans.

Dirty humans.

Smelly humans.

A green dot appeared in the centre of the purple circle. His date had arrived. Casting his mind back to the many hours spent hooked up to his green dot, he stumbled. This was it. In the flesh. Warm and tactile.

He scanned the tables for a new arrival, but all he could see was a bunch of normal people. Nobody shone. Nobody radiated attractiveness so charged with promise they couldn't be resisted. The scene in front of him was mundane. A few steps closer and he would be exposed to his waiting companion.

He faltered, paused in the middle of the pavement while the throbbing mass of humanity passed either side of him.

Abruptly, he turned.

The green dot in the purple circle stayed still while he walked away, gradually gathering pace. And then the dot started moving towards him, following him. He must have got closer than he thought. The memories came back, only this time it was the memory of the button turning orange, of his virtual companion agreeing to meet in the flesh.

He turned to face the restaurant. An ordinary-looking middle-aged man dressed in jeans and a brown jacket was walking towards him, smiling. The green dot kept pace with his approach.

Eyes, limbs and lips – the man was real.

Something inside him melted. He smiled back, switched off his device, tucked it into his pocket and walked towards the ordinary man that had turned his heart.

# PLACODERMI PROTECTION

Two hundred babies slide from their artificial wombs into fleshy gel-filled pods. How I wish they could stay in their amniotic homes, but we need them and today it's my turn to keep watch.

A tear forms in the corner of my eye. They won't live long. They won't be remembered. And yet, they're the next link in the long expanding chain of evolution.

In the womb we manipulated them and, unlike the rest of us, they know what it's like to be one of our ancient aquatic ancestors, an armoured fish, one of the Placodermi brought back from extinction.

As soon as they enter their pods, this new batch of boys and girls, full of ancient instinct, begin firing their neurons. The gel translates and transmits the signals to the tech we've implanted in the re-engineered Placodermi that protect the fragile coral. Our babies drive the fish at the bottom of the ocean.

I pull on the watcher's headset and immediately I'm as immersed in their world as they are. I love watching them ease into their new environment, from artificial womb to the pod and the deep sea. I only wish I could keep them safe.

I can't.

In the distance, sediment from the ocean floor is disturbed. The first attack of the day has started. It might be today's first, but they've been attacking for a hundred years and although we know they come for the coral, we don't know why. We only know we must do everything we can to protect it so it can regrow.

A solid mass of enemy crab-bots churn the ocean bed as they approach.

Our babies turn gracefully inside their sinisterly beautiful virtual bodies.

You could be forgiven for mistaking the choreographed shoal for an underwater ballet. But, if you were their enemy, you'd be cruelly deceived. Up close, the hard scaly bodies and sharp teeth reveal what a formidable foe these ancient fish are. What an excellent choice of ancestor to bring back from extinction.

It's horrible to hear the painful cacophony of crying from the pods as these gorgeous babies prepare for the attack, despite their deep-rooted instinctual fear.

An enemy crab-bot drifts away from the pack and propels itself slowly towards our brave shoal. It sinks to the floor and edges sideways. I saw this the last time I was on watch a couple of weeks ago. At first it was one or two, and then the whole pack made a sudden shift and scurried along the ocean bed. About half of them made it through and began mining the coral before being torn apart or chased away by our babies.

A high-pitched scream pierces through the crying from the pods. One of the Placodermi dashes towards the crab-bot faster than I've ever seen. It opens its jaw and clamps down on the bot with a twisting movement, slamming it into a nearby rock. The scream reaches a fever pitch.

And then the bot explodes.

The screaming stops dead.

The feedback loop from fish to gel to baby must have transferred the trauma from the explosion to the pod.

The gel seeps out into the drain and the pod opens.

The baby boy is dead. It happens. I hate it, but it happens.

A loud alarm reminds me that I must harvest his sperm and get it to the lab before it's too late.

We need more babies like him.

We must protect the coral.

At all costs.

# RESPONSES FROM
# THE EXPERTS

Claire Steves
Clinical academic Deputy Director of TwinsUK and Consultant
Geriatrician at Guys and St Thomas's Hospital
Response to "Zygosity Saves the Day"

I think the title of this moving piece should really be 'Compassion saves the day'. Human compassion – from one person, Lara, to another, Beatrice. Their love enables them to beat the system.

Sadly, the frightening future medical system in which they live is far from compassionate: removing freedom from the old and infirm, and passing judgement on individuals because of their past choices. The story shows how even apparently beneficial endeavours – such as understanding how to help an individual to remain healthy into old age – can be misused if we are not careful.

In our lab we are motivated to try to understand why some older adults become frail and suffer, as Beatrice does, from cognitive and physical decline, and why others appear to escape. By understanding these differences, we hope to unlock mechanisms by which to personalise medicine to an individual's own risks. Currently, the average woman spends 19 years at the end of her life with her function limited in some way. Men spend only fractionally less. Our mission is to try to reduce this, increasing healthspan in the same way we have increased lifespan.

Yet as this story so poignantly illustrates, even if we were able to achieve this, not everyone would be in the right place at the right time to take advantage of it. How would a compassionate system cope with that? How can our science help pave the way for its better usage?

Firstly, and fundamentally, research in labs like our own needs to continue to be publicly available and widely disseminated. Openness and lack of secrecy in research reduces the chance that good ideas are only exploitable by private entities – in this case private healthcare insurance companies. Thankfully, key medical research funders such as ours make this a condition of their funding.

Secondly, we need to do more research to understand how technologies are taken up by different groups and different personalities (such as Beatrice and Lara), and learn how to ensure a fairer gain from advances in science, whoever you are.

Science and knowledge can only go so far, however. To design a fair society, we need the 'veil of ignorance'. Philosophers hundreds of years ago understood that our wider systems (including the health system) need to work from everyone's standpoint. To that end, John Rawls created the thought experiment where the engineers of society were 'veiled' as to what place they were to hold in that society, i.e. whether they ended up as Lara or Beatrice.

Such a compassionate system could yet save the day.

Danbee Kim

Neuroscientist on the verge of earning a PhD and collaborator on
*The Queen's Heart* and *Zenith*

As a scientist, I tend to fall in love with science fiction that reminds me of the human consequences of science. This might seem strange, because often the human consequences are dark, dystopian, and depressing; however, because I worry that today's scientists aren't worried enough, I love these stories for speaking the truth that many scientists would rather ignore.

We are blinded by illusions of a perfectly objective science.

When I decided to conduct neuroscience research in cuttlefish, it was because I found their beautiful strangeness so inspiring – here was a creature that, in many ways, couldn't be more different from us humans... And yet, not only did they display incredible complexity and coordination in their nervous system, but I also felt a connection to them, a mind-to-mind connection that transcended all of our physical differences. Surely I would have no trouble convincing the neuroscience community that cuttlefish are worthy of our attention.

In words, many agreed. In deeds, however, doing any kind of neuroscience research on species that are not mouse, rat, zebrafish or fly is an enormous practical challenge.

These short stories highlight so well how our convergence as a scientific community on such a small sample of the brains and cognitive organisations, given our incredibly diverse and multi-flavoured world, is an enormous disadvantage. The narrowing of animal models, as they are called, that scientific research systems currently support and encourage also narrows our insights and perspective on what is possible for our own minds.

Of course, there are many fighting the good fight, seeing the value of diversity in what we study, in who does the studying, and willingly moving past the easy paths of fast results and trophy publications. But it's not easy to be the few in any research institution who are willing to ask the questions that we all know *should* be asked, but are too tedious, too philosophical, too dangerous to the status quo.

Maybe I've become cynical.

Something that gives me hope is the open science movement, the open access publishing movement, and the citizen science movement. These challenges to tradition are not just a good idea – they are essential to our future as thinking beings.

'Be curious' – I've heard this phrase said so many times, to myself, to school children, to the elderly, to young technocrats who have become millionaires at 26 but still don't know how to be happy. They are wonderful words, but if we want them to mean anything, then we have to roll up our sleeves and remind ourselves: fancy technology and prestigious publications will not solve our problems. Hard-working humans who acknowledge how subjective, how painstakingly slow, how *human* the endeavour of building, organising and sharing knowledge is and needs to be – *that* will be the beginning of solving our problems, and the first step for anyone who truly wants to be curious.

Liviu Babitz
CEO & Co-Founder of Cyborg Nest

We decide which story to tell, we decide which questions we ask, and most importantly, we decide what we do with the answers. The future can easily be proposed with a taste of bitterness, a taste of something will go wrong, but will it? It is comfortably realistic to assume it will actually be amazing, positive and constructive, simply because the past proves that we, as a species, are doing better every few generations. People cry for the past to return, but we forget that a few decades ago we had apartheid, we had half of Europe behind a big lock, global poverty rates were much higher, and we lived 10 to 15 years less. That is not during prehistoric times; that is just a few years ago.

But what am I trying to say? That it is all positive and amazing? No, because it is not. We do make mistakes, and we have to learn from them. More than that: the more we ask and learn before we push Play, the fewer mistakes we make. We need to make the right decisions. It is never about Yes or No; rather, it is about How. Oh, one more thing: let's not forget to smile and enjoy the ride…

# ACKNOWLEDGEMENTS

With thanks to all those who inspired the stories and helped form them into what they are, in particular my beta readers to whom this collection is dedicated. Thanks also to Allen Ashley and the Clockhouse London Writers, the Virtual Futures team, the various scientists and future-tech folk that I've worked with on collaborative projects and those that have inspired from afar. Not forgetting Beverly and Deborah who allowed me to spend time with them at TwinsUK. Finally, and with special thanks, those wonderful people who have contributed their wise words to the collection – Christine Aicardi, Claire Steves, Danbee Kim, and Liviu Babitz.

*Dormant Status* originally published in the anthology, *Fairy Tales and Folklore Re-imagined*, Between The Lines Publishing
*I Am Blue* originally published in *Speculative 66* issue 9
*Syrup and Cigarettes* originally published as *Breaking the Rules Is Not Allowed* in Fictional Pairings
*Zygosity Saves the Day* originally published by King's College London as part of the Strange Brains, Alien Minds project
*The Never-Ending Nanobot Nectar* originally published in *Virtual Futures Near-Future Fictions Vol. 1*
*Happy Forever Day* originally published in *Linux Developer & User* magazine
*The Blockchain Blues* originally published in *Linux Developer & User* magazine
*Placodermi Protection* originally published in *Far Horizons* magazine

# ALSO BY STEPHEN ORAM

*Quantum Confessions*

"A veritable head trip; yet rooted in a believable and sometimes visceral near-future."

Grey is a high performer with attitude. Aled is torn between his morals and his desires. They live in a world where those who believe in absolute truth are on a collision course with those who don't. Society is becoming dangerously polarised and despite a thread of history that binds Aled and Grey together they take opposite sides in the conflict; Grey is recruited by The Project and Aled is given custody of The Proof of Existence.

Against the backdrop of a failing society and experiments to find the link between quantum physics and a supreme being, the real question that unfolds is...

"Who chooses your reality?"

*Fluence*

Imagine a world where your influence on social media determines your job, your home and your friends. A world without politicians, where the corporations run the country.

Set in a dystopian London, *Fluence* is a story of aspiration and desperation and of power seen and unseen. Amber is young and ambitious. Martin is burnt out by years of struggling. She cheats to get what she wants while he barely clings on to what he has.

It's the week before the annual Pay Day when strata positions are decided by the algorithms. The social media feed is frenetic with people trying to boost their influence rating, while those above the strata and those who've opted out pursue their own manipulative goals.

To what extremes, and at what cost to their families, will Amber and Martin go to achieve the Fluence they desire?

The story in this collection, *Connections Count*, is set in the world of *Fluence*.

*Eating Robots*

The future is ours and it's up for grabs...

Step into a high-tech vision of the future with author of *Quantum Confessions* and *Fluence* Stephen Oram. Featuring health-monitoring mirrors, tele-empathic romances and limb-repossessing bailiffs, *Eating Robots* explores the collision of utopian dreams and twisted realities in a world where humanity and technology are becoming ever more intertwined.

Sometimes funny, often unsettling, and always with a word of warning, these thirty sci-fi shorts will stay with you long after you've turned the final page.